AF668091

BEST OF SHERLOCK HOLMES

10 Sensational Crime Thrillers

Retold *By*

M K Parthasarathy

UNICORN BOOKS

Publishers
UNICORN BOOKS

F-2/16, Ansari Road, Daryaganj, New Delhi-110002
E-mail: info@unicornbooks.in • *Website:* www.unicornbooks.in
☎ 011-23275434, 23262683

Branch: *Mumbai*
23-25, Zaoba Wadi Thakurdwar, Mumbai-400002
☎ 022-22010941, 022-22053387
E-mail: rapidex@bom5.vsnl.net.in

© **Copyright:** Unicorn Books

ISBN 978-81-7806-199-3

Best of Sherlock Holmes

Edition: 2015

All rights reserved. No part of this publication may be reproduced, stored in a retrieval system or transmitted, in any form or by any means, electronic, mechanical, photocopying, recording or otherwise, without the prior permission in writing from the Author/ Publisher. Anybody doing so shall face legal action and will be liable for damages.

Printed at : Param Offsetters, Okhla, New Delhi-110020

SIR ARTHUR CONAN DOYLE

(May 22, 1859 – July 7, 1930)

Conan Doyle's two sides of life are rather contrary! On the professional side he was a doctor and on the personal side he was a prolific writer of crime fictions.

Born in Edinburgh in 1859, Conan Doyle was an academic don. He had finished his doctorate from the Edinburgh University in 1885. Though he had set up his practice, he never charged the poor. Instead, he helped them buy medicines and bare essentials until they recuperated.

It needed more funds. So during his spare time, he began writing. Since he had the natural talent for writing crime fictions – which was seldom in those days – by creating an imaginary character called Sherlock Holmes as a detective he tried a title, *'A Scandal In Bohemia,'* featuring Holmes as a private dick which emerged victorious and laid a red carpet welcome for him to spread his wings.

People who never tasted a crime thriller until then found his works very thrilling. Not only in the British soil, but world wide his stories became a mega hit. With name and fame, Conan Doyle continued to write. He had written four full length novels and 56 short stories, with Holmes as the master detective. His collection of 56 short stories fall under five categories.

Conan Doyle had no parallel and his works have been filmed too, apart from stage plays and cartoon quips. Some of the modern days Best Selling authors like James Hadley Chase too had quoted the name of Holmes in their works.

That the names of Conan Doyle and his successful creations Sherlock Holmes as well as Dr Watson rippled out across many generations and withstood the weather of time even after 120 years now, speak volume that these stories are immortal and will continue to reign the heart of the people even after many decades.

It was in July 1930 that Conan Doyle breathed his last.

CONTENT

A Scandal In Bohemia

On a dark, breezy night during the third week of March 1888, Dr Watson was returning home after visiting a patient. The horse-drawn cart in which he was travelling now, nearly gouged its way amidst the evening jay walkers who hurriedly shifted to one side on hearing the rhythmic beating of the horse's hooves or sighting it.

The clouds had obliterated even the sickle of moon up in the sky. A few in the crowd there in Bohemia, who knew Dr Watson, waved and he acknowledged. He knew he had become popular there not because of his profession, but because of his association with his detective friend, Sherlock Holmes.

Dr Watson's lips spontaneously curved into a smile at the thought of Sherlock Holmes. It was high time he had met him. After he had got married, he seldom found time for that. Knowing this, Holmes too did not bother to call on him.

Dr Watson pulled out the chain-watch and glanced at it. It was 7.20 p.m. The evening was still young. He told the coach attendant to go through the Baker Street where Holmes lived. The coach paused before the house. Through the glass window Dr Watson could see the mobile silhouette of Holmes as he paced up and down in his study room. It could mean one thing: he was mentally busy! When wasn't he?

Getting down he went in, ushered by Holmes' servant maid. At the sight of him, Holmes beamed. "What a surprise! Is it my dear friend, Dr Watson or I'm imagining things?" Dr Watson smiled for an answer, realising that he had missed his friend's company in the recent days.

"Take the weight off your feet, Watson," Holmes said, "After your marriage I can see you've become thicker in the middle!" Dr Watson sat on his usual seat next to Holmes, mentally appreciating his sentiments that he did not shift it from there all these days. "Anything cooking?" he asked. "Are you working on any case? It now bores me without your company!" Dr Watson meant what he said.

"Are you really interested? If so, you've come at the right time. Here, read it before I tell you what it is all about." Holmes gave him an envelope. Dr Watson fished out a letter from it.

It read:

"*Dear Mr Holmes:*

Your recent, praiseworthy successful investigation for the Royal Houses of Europe - this account of yours we have from all quarters received. A gentleman will call on you at 7.45 p.m. today. This case is to be treated on a par with the previous one with secrecy.

The visiting client will be wearing a mask. Please don't get curious to know who he's. Be ready to receive him and render your best services.

–Thanks.

"Why the visitor chose to remain mysterious?" asked Dr Watson for something to say.

Holmes went and sat opposite to him. "Obviously to conceal his identity!" he went on, "Any way, it is our duty to unearth that one too. To start with, what can you make out of this letter, I mean, the paper the writer had used?" Dr Watson turned the paper in his hands and saw. "Well, all that I can make out is, it's a costly paper," he replied.

"Hold it under the light and see."

He did as he was told. Now he could see some odd alphabets in it. He saw the capital 'E' and small 'g,' and capital 'P' and 'G,' with the back drop of small 't.' "Could it be the manufacturer's emblem?" he voiced his doubt.

"No. The capital 'G' and small 't' stand for *Gesellscraft.* It's a German word for a firm as we abbreviate a company as Co. 'P' denotes *Papier.* And that 'Eg,' for *Egria,* I mean, a country where German language is spoken," decoded Holmes after verifying from an old and worn-out, bulky *Continental Gazetteer* which he always kept handy.

"I think this letter was written by a German, wasn't it?" asked Dr Watson.

"That's right. He had used a Bohemian Paper. Moreover, these Germans are known for their crude language. The sentence with the wordage that, '*This account of yours we have from all quarters received!*' endorses that it was written by a German."

Just then they heard the sound of a cart pull up. "Here he comes," said the doctor. Moments later, the mysterious visitor swept in. He was a stalwart. He'd be any age between 25 and 30, tall and heavily built with square indented chin and aggressive jaws. He wore a hat, the brim of it extending like Saturn's rings and his masked face glared at them. "You got my note?" he asked bluntly eyeing the two.

"Welcome," said Holmes as he indicated a chair for him. The visitor eyed the doctor before he spoke up. "I told you the matter is urgent and strictly confidential. I want to talk to you private, Mr Holmes."

"By the way, meet my friend Dr Watson," Holmes went on to introduce him as he grabbed his hand and pushed him back in the chair when he made an attempt to go out. "He assists me in all my cases. If I were the body of the investigations, he's the soul to it. So, you can take him into concerts as you trust me, Mr.....Aw.... "

"I'm a noble man of Bohemia. You can call me Count Von Kramm although I'm not entitled to be called so. And I've orders from my employer to wear this mask."

"I guessed so," nodded Holmes.

"Obviously, the case I'm going to refer to you requires utmost caution and top secret. It concerns the well-being of the dynasty king of Bohemia at the great House of Ormstein. Hence, we leave nothing to chance!" he disclosed.

"I guessed that one too, your majesty!" smiled Holmes.

On hearing the word *Majesty,* the masked visitor looked at them sharply. "Well, before I tell you what it's all about, let me come out in the open!" So saying he sprang to his feet and took off his mask and stood staring at Holmes, expecting him to get surprised.

But on seeing the *I-had-already-guessed-who-you-are* expression on Holmes' face, it was now his turn to look surprised! "When I insist on top secret," he added matter-of-fact, "I mustn't withhold anything. I'm a royal descent of the king of Bohemia, better known as Wilhem Gottareich Sigismond Von Ormstein, the grand duke of Castle-Falstein!"

"Thanks for your open approach, though as I said, I'd already guessed that. You can rely on us. We always maintain our guarantee of secrecy. Please go ahead," encouraged Holmes.

"Well, to begin with, I'm in a spot! Like any other adolescent I too was in love with a girl and even took photograph with her too. This was when I was 25 years of age. Now I'm 30. After some months I'd found out that she was no match for me. We had different views. I tried my best to adjust, but it wouldn't work out. Finally, we parted. But now she's trying to dent my reputation. She's using the photograph and my letters as a lever to blackmail me. But mind you Mr Holmes, her idea is not to extract money, but to get even with me."

"How?"

"Well, I'm getting married. The bride is the second daughter of the Scandinavian king, princess Clotide Lothman von Saxe-Meningen. So, I needn't elaborate what would become of it if they come to know about this past. Even if there's an iota of doubt, it'd wipe out the marriage proposal clean as a whistle!"

"You haven't married her. And there's no concrete evidence except for these letters and photograph of yours. We can always argue that the letters are forged and photograph too fabricated, can't we?" pointed out Sherlock Holmes.

"Not a chance. It's not my photo alone. The one I'd taken with her. And the local studio man will be a key witness to it. Yet, I tried my best to recover them. I, thrice, had her house burgled and twice arranged with the thugs to have her waylaid. But we couldn't seize them from her. I don't figure where she's hiding it. Either with her lawyer or at the bank safety vault. But then no lady will leave such things with a third person, nor at the bank vault which can be robbed. So, it's apparent she's too clever to be fooled," the visiting king said at length.

"What puzzles me is, why is she not carrying it with her? Is the photograph a framed one to hang on the wall? I mean, is it a cabinet sized?"

"Come to think of it, yes."

"I'll see what best I can do. Give me a week's time, will you?" said Holmes.

"One week is too long. I've hardly three days left for my marriage engagement. As she's planning to send them on the day of the betrothal, you'll have to act fast!"

"There are two ways: either abduct the woman for a few days till you get married, or go after them. Let me try the second way, first," smiled Holmes. And it made the king too chuckle at Holmes' crafty suggestion.

"Try the second way, first, Mr Holmes," he put a bulky hand bag on the table and added, "You'll find 300 pounds in gold and 700 in currencies. This is only a retainer. If you get me what I want, I wonder why I shouldn't give a province of my kingdom to you!"

Holmes handed a receipt to it as he asked him the name and address of the woman.

"Mademoiselle Irene Adler staying at Briony lodge, Serpentine Avenue, St. John's wood!"

That afternoon at 3, Dr Watson went to Holmes' house as planned earlier. The servant maid told him that Holmes had left home at 8 in the morning and not returned yet. He waited in the study room, their usual rendezvous. Minutes later, a tall and well-built man, with a French-cut beard and long hairs breezed in. He winked at the waiting doctor and went inside the bedroom. Even to Dr Watson the disguise that Holmes was wearing looked so genuine. Ten minutes later he came back in his normal self and sat before his friend.

"I bet you had a tough time?"

"Yes, at Briony lodge," Holmes went on smiling, "I hung on there near a row of stables, helped the horse man who gave me two pence and casually enquired around about Irene Adler. They say she's a beautiful woman, a singer at music concerts.

She seems to live by the clock. Leaves her room at 5 in the evening and returns in time for dinner. Otherwise she doesn't go anywhere. However, she has a male visitor called Godfrey Norton. He lives at Inner Temple and visits her twice a day."

"What's the relationship between them?"

"This man Norton is a lawyer. His entry now widens my investigations. If he's a fiancé of hers, then the chances of her leaving the photo in his custody is more. Now I've to keep a tab on this man also. As I was brooding over, a cab pulled up there and a well-dressed handsome man got out and stormed inside. After about half an hour he came out and hopped into the coach, urging the driver to rush to the church at St. Monica. "Before that, go to Gross and Hankey's in Regent street. Snap it up and earn an incentive of half a guinea!" I heard him say to the coachman. And with that he was gone.

"Just then Irene Alder came out. She waved at a passing coach and told the man to dash to the same church at St. Monica! I didn't spend much time ruminating my choices. I too engaged a coach and went after them. After paying the coachman I stormed inside the church and saw a clergyman, Adler woman and Norton inside. Except for these three, the church was practically empty. I sat in a bench as if I was a wanderer. At once, Norton rushed to me saying them that I was god-sent, because they — Irene Adler and Godfrey Norton — were getting married and they needed a witness!"

"Earned any more extra pounds there, too?" the doctor put in jovially.

"You bet. She gave a sovereign as a souvenir, telling me to wear it in my watch strap. Once outside, she told Norton he could find her in the park at 5 in the evening and they went back separately. That's all there's to it at the moment. Anyway, we've got some important work near Briony lodge at 7 p.m. when she returns," said Homes.

"What's that?"

"To find out where she's hidden the photograph, I guess, I've to enact a drama with your help. All that you've to do is to come and stand outside the lodge, pay no attention to what happens to me there and, finally when you see the windows being thrown open and finding me lying on the bed inside and raise my hand and give a signal, toss an object I'll be giving you through the window and raise an alarm as, 'Fire.' There ends your part. After that, go to the corner of the street and wait for me. I'll join you in ten minutes."

"What's that object? Will it burst?"

"Not at all. It's something like a smoke screen."

"Okay, but why you tell me to turn my blind eye to what happens to you there?"

"That's part of the plan," said Holmes, getting to his feet.

Shortly after 6.30, Holmes, wearing the disguise of a clergyman with a long beard and a Bible in hand, stood before the mirror and admired his image. Then they left.

The location of the Brion lodge was exactly as Holmes had described it before. There were people of all classes: vagabonds sitting at one corner while well-dressed men and women go past up and down. At 7 p.m. sharp the coach that usually takes Alder woman came and pulled up. At once one of the vagabonds rushed to her to help her carry her things. Meanwhile, another darted to her for the same purpose. This fierce competition between them ensued in a wordy duel and snowballed into fist fight!

On seeing this, the guards standing at another corner of the road, ran up to the fighting men. Now there was more exchange of fist fight. Irene Alder, who got down, stood frozen with fear. At this juncture, Holmes, in the disguise of the clergyman, dashed to them as if intervening, lurched then fell down clutching his face which was bleeding now!

It rattled the fighting men. They fled from the spot. Alder woman saw the wounded clergyman. The onlookers ran to his help. "He's dead," one of them said. "No, not dead, but injured, bleeding profusely," said another.

Irene Alder felt sorry for the clergyman. It was to save her that he had intervened and now got hurt. She wanted to help him out. "Bring him in, will you?" she told the men who stood crowding the clergyman. Moments later, the clergyman was carried inside. Dr Watson stood watching the fun, wondering how Holmes was going to manage, his hand absent-mindedly fingering the object given by Holmes with an instruction to hurl it through the window the moment it is opened.

Dr Watson saw the outline of Holmes propping up on the bed and the others moving about. Then someone threw the windows open. The doctor saw Holmes lift his right hand. It was the signal! At once he yanked out the object, a plumber's smoke rocket with a cap on both the ends. It resembled a cigar. He tossed it through the window and shouted, 'Fire!' The next moment, a column of smoke drifted from it and enveloped the room.

The smoke and the shout of 'Fire' added tension. Dr Watson saw the inmates running about in utter confusion. Then he slowly walked away to the street corner to wait for his friend.

Ten minutes later, the clergyman joined him. Together they hired a coach and went back to their room in Baker's street. As Holmes was unlocking the door, a passerby wished to him, "Good night, Mr Holmes!"

"I wonder how anyone recognised me with this disguise, or someone drunk enough to see none but I live here," said Holmes as they moved in. Once inside, he took Dr Watson's hand in his and appreciated him saying that he did a good job of it.

When asked by his friend how it all went, Holmes spoke up, "My psychology move paid dividend, Dr Watson…"

"If so, have you brought the photo the king asked for?"

"Not yet. But I know where she's hiding it. I told you, I'd make her show the spot.

The moment there was this fire alarm from you as well as by the others with smoke drifting inside, they all got rattled. When there's a fire or an earthquake, the reaction of the people will be to save their most valuable things. A mother wants to save her child, an unmarried girl wants to save her jewels. Likewise, Irene Alder wanted to save the photo. As I had figured, she at once rushed to the secret recess at the back of a sliding panel over the bell-pull. I saw her take the photo out.

"Since I did not want her to shift it elsewhere, I bawled saying that it was a false alarm. Only then she saw the smouldering rocket, put the photo back in its place and left the room. I quickly got up, wondering whether or not to take the photo with me. Just then her coachman stormed inside. So, I gave up the idea and came out. However, as a first thing tomorrow, soon after dawn, let's take the king with us and go there. Before Irene Alder could get up, we'll hang on there under the pretence of waiting for her to get up. This will convince her servant maid. When she loses interest in us, let's take the photo and bolt. Now let me write to the king, asking him to be present here early in the morning."

It seemed a good idea to Dr Watson. As told by Holmes, he stayed with him that night. At the crack of dawn, the restless king called on them. He looked excited. Holmes narrated to him all that had happened. He also added how she got married to Godfrey Norton and how he (Holmes) had seconded their wedding at the church the previous day. Then the three of them set off to Briony lodge in a coach.

But there awaited a disappointment for the duo. The servant maid's eyebrows shot up quizzically. "Is it Mr Sherlock Holmes?" she said, "My mistress Irene and her husband Mr Norton had left for the Continent by the 5.15 train this morning. They had gone to settle in England. Before leaving, she said she would call in ....."

"If so, my papers?" blurted out the king, his voice betraying his anxiety.

Holmes went past the servant maid and reached the secret spot behind the bell-pull and fished out an envelope and a photo wrapped with newspapers. On tearing the wrapper they got a jolt! This person in the photo was Irene Herself ! Holmes tore open the envelope and extracted a letter. It was addressed to Holmes by Irene Alder.

"*Dear Mr Sherlock Holmes:*

At the outset, I must put in black and white that you did a remarkable thing. You almost had me fooled.

I nearly fell for the drama enacted by you. It was a nice idea that you wore the disguise of a clergyman. But mind you, I had been warned months before that if at all the king engages anyone, it must be you. And they have given me your address too. So, since then I've been cautious. Yesterday, after you've pointed out that the fire call was a hoax, I left the spot, but sent my coachman to keep an eye on you. His presence deterred you from helping yourself with the hidden photo. You forget I'm an actor and that I put disguise too. Hence, it didn't take long for me to know your real identity. However, to convince myself, I wore the disguise of a man and tailed you back home and wished you good night when you were unlocking the front door.

Mr Holmes, by the time you get this letter, I'll have gone miles away with my husband, a better match to me than the king. Please tell him that. Anyway, I'm taking the photo and the letter of the king — the two things you were after — with me. It's a precautionary measure.You do not know about the king. He's a bit vindictive. So, any time he tries to give me trouble, I know what to do with the photo and the letter. Precisely, if he leaves me alone, I'll leave him alone. That's it.

Finally, I must add this: I don't fret, nor do I've any ill-feeling about you. After all, you've done your duty. And come to think of it, I admire you the way you carried on your investigation. It's par excellence.

Closing with regards

Most Sincerely

Irene Norton

"A pro-active lady!" remarked Dr Watson, after reading the letter.

But the king looked pleased. He thanked Holmes and Dr Watson for their intervention that ensured there wouldn't be any trouble from Irene and that the king could go ahead and get married without any fear. "Now what shall I give you Mr Holmes? How about a province of my kingdom?" asked the king.

"I'd rather settle for the photo of Irene in your hand. And nothing else."

"Why you want her photo?"

"I'd keep it as a memento from the lady who didn't fall for my gimmick," said Holmes as he put Irene's photo in his coat pocket.

The king regarded Holmes for some time, then he shook hands with the two before he turned and walked away to his waiting coach.

The duo watched him go, then turned and glanced around. A brightly-lit restaurant athwart the road seemed to be inviting. The two went towards it, mentally planning what to eat there!

The Boscombe Valley Mystery

"Dear Dr Watson:

If I'm not dragging you away from home, would you meet me at Paddington railway station at 11.15? There's something cooking at the western side of England that needs our immediate attention. The atmosphere there is fine with sun and air." – Holmes.

Dr Watson had just then finished his morning meal. He glanced at his wife with a quizzical stare. Knowing the sign, Mrs Watson told him to go ahead. "A change of scene is what you require now after the monotonous work for months together. In your absence our Anstruther will manage the show here," she spoke encouragingly.

Dr Watson was a retired army doctor. The strict discipline with which he had served, kept him in perfect trim. And he always made it a point to keep the travel bag well-equipped for an immediate take off. Hence, in just 15 minutes he stepped inside the deserted Paddington railway station.

Minutes later, he and Holmes were sitting comfortably in the train when Holmes plunged into the subject. "I suppose this Boscombe Valley Mystery has become a complicated murder case. The place, Boscombe, is a district situated a little distance from Herefordshire. There were two aged good friends. They have many things in common. Both returned from Australia after making a lot of money there and bought more properties here. One of them by name, Mr John Turner, had let a farm of his to Mr Charles Mc Carthy. Of the two, the former was rich. Yet they met and spent their time in each other's company. While Turner had a daughter, McCarthy had a son. Both the children, deprived of their mothers, were in their late teens. McCarthy had a couple of servants while Turner had many. That's their background."

"Here comes the problem. Late Monday, on 3rd June, around 3 p.m. McCarthy went to the Boscombe pool as he was having an appointment there. The distance from his residence, Hatherley, to the pool is about two furlongs. He was seen going past by two people: a gamekeeper called William Crowder and an old woman. Minutes after that, the same two saw his son, James go after his father carrying a gun in hand. That's all these eyewitnesses could say. Later they learned that McCarthy was dead, hit on the head with an hard object, may be by the butt of a gun. Meanwhile, another eyewitness, the 14-year-old daughter of the Boscombe Valley Estate's game-keeper endorses this theory. According to her, the father and son had a wordy duel and that the son had lifted his hand to strike the old man. Frightened, the girl ran back home and narrated to her parents what she had seen. Soon James rushed to them and sought their help, crying that his father had been killed by some one. However, they all rushed to the site and saw Mc Carthy lying dead, bleeding from the severe head injury. That's it. And it points an accusing finger at James and he was taken into custody."

"Wouldn't it be a circumstantial evidence, taking things on the face value?" pointed out Dr Watson. "Of course," nodded Holmes, "When there's no other source of knowing the truth. But if one reads between the lines, the hidden truth will come to surface. This youth, James, didn't protest when they arrested him. Here, read the story which appeared in the local newspaper."

Dr Watson took the *Herefordshire daily* and glanced at the true confession made by James to the police. In his statement James had declared that he was away for three days and came back only on 3rd morning. His father wasn't at home when he arrived. Then he saw him get down from the coach with Ross, their servant, and started walking away. Not knowing where his father was heading for, James took his gun and went to the Boscombe pool towards the rabbit-warren. It was a coincidence that James too was heading in the same direction where his father had gone. It was at this juncture, that the gamekeeper Crowder saw him go. Suddenly James heard his father scream 'Cooee'! It was a sign between them to call each other! Wondering how his father who did not even know his arrival back home, knew that he (James) was coming after him to call him thus.

"The sight of James materialising from nowhere took his father off guard. He shouted at James, because McCarthy was an ill-tempered man. They disputed on certain matters, then James left. Here, the eyewitness girl says that she saw James lifting his gun holding hand in an attempt to strike his father. At once she had fled. After James had gone about 200 feet he heard his father's scream in agony. He rushed back and saw him lying amidst a pool of blood from the wound on his head. He squatted down and placed his father's head in his lap when the aged man mumbled 'Rat....' before he dropped dead. After that, James darted to Crowder and sought his help. That's all there's to his account. However, when later he was picked up by the police and produced before the coroner, James, in his reply to the coroner's queries, said he couldn't make out his father's dying declaration and that about the argument, he refused to comment on it. It annoyed the coroner.

"To another query how come his father shouted 'cooee' even before seeing him, James said he had no idea. James went on to say that he remembers having seen something like a grey-coloured coat or cloth lying about 10 yards away from where his father's body was and that after his back was turned to that while he was attending to his father, someone must've sneaked in there and taken it with him for he didn't see it when he darted to seek help.

"It concluded that James was guilty as he was hiding what he argued about with his father and that his shouting 'cooee' even before seeing James, was contrary. And hence the coroner came down heavily on James and instantly sent him to jail."

"Looks like an open and shut case to me," Dr Watson opined. Holmes shook his head, "I'd rather disagree. I've a feeling that James wasn't guilty. Let me expose the truth!" As a next move, around 4 p.m. the duo went to Stroud Valley where the elegant country Ross stood. There they saw inspector Lestrade waiting for them. While they were having a tea that Lestrade said it was clear that James was the murderer. Just then a pretty young girl came in and dotted before them. "Good afternoon, gentlemen," she went on looking at Holmes, "I'm Mr Turner's daughter. James and I were very good friends from our childhood days. I know James personally than anybody else. I swear he wouldn't have done such a thing. It's good that you've intervened, Mr Holmes. Please probe and you'll find out that the police is wrong and free James if you can. When you go to see James in the jail, please tell him that I believe his story and not the police version."

"I will do that," assured Holmes. Shifting her gaze to Lestrade, she addressed to him, "That's master detective Sherlock Holmes. See, he believes my theory." Lestrade smiled dryly, "Maybe he doesn't want to hurt your sentiments."

To Holmes, she said, "About the so-called argument between the father and son, it's about me! His father Mr McCarthy wanted us to get married. But we moved like brother and sister. Moreover, he's younger to me. This quite often erupted in an argument! To tell one more fact, my father, Mr Turner was against it!."

"Can I have a word with your father?"

"I'm sorry, Mr Holmes. The doctor wouldn't allow anyone to see him. According to doctor Willows, my father's feeble with a broken down nervous system. None but Mr McCarthy knows my father because they both were serving in Victoria, Australia years before!" On hearing this Holmes' eyes sparkled, "I take it was while working in the gold mines there your father had accumulated his wealth. Right?" The girl nodded. "Thanks for this piece of information. It'll help me probe the case," Holmes smiled. The girl then excused herself and ran back.

Shortly after that, Holmes and Lestrade went to the railway station to see James in the jail, leaving Dr Watson behind. Left alone, Dr Watson, as a medical officer, analysed the head injury sustained by McCarthy. The post mortem report said that the left side of his head was severely damaged due to a heavy blow, because the posterior third of the left parietal bone as well as the left occipital bone's left side had been shattered. This could be possible only when hitting from behind and not from the front side as the eye witness girl had said that she saw James aim a blow while facing his father! He decided to tell about his observation to Holmes.

Holmes and Lestrade took their time to return. "My meeting with James didn't help much. Either he's still dazed or he must be covering the murderer. And a few years ago when she was at the boarding school and he at Bristol, he had married a bar maid. So he was away for three days. Now finding that he had landed in serious trouble, the barmaid wife of his had given him a brush off, stating that she'd join her other husband in Bermuda Dockyard. Maybe, this secret marriage had triggered off an argument between him and his father. However, his father must be pleased that James' secret wedding snapped."

"But that doesn't answer the puzzle. Who knocked out McCarthy?" asked Dr Watson. "Could be anyone whom McCarthy had an appointment to discuss something at the pool. Second, his shouting 'cooee' could be to notify his location to the person he was going to meet there. Then they returned to the lodge. The next morning around 9, Lestrade arrived in a coach and took Holmes and Dr Watson to Boscombe pool in Hatherley. "I'm told that the old man Turner is sinking. He was so magnanimous to let McCarthy have the Heatherley farm without rent. A man about whom people there spoke so high of."

Heatherley farm was a two-storied building with upstairs quarters too. The maid who answered the bell took the three inside. Holmes' eagle eyes missed nothing, including the shoes McCarthy wore at the time of his death. From there they proceeded to the Boscombe pool which was hardly about 50 yards in between the Turner's park and the Heatherley farm house, surrounded by woodland. Holmes squatted down and examined the spot indicated by Lestrade where McCarthy's body was found. He then ran around the pool in knee deep waters before returning to the spot again. When asked why was he running in the waters, Holmes said that he wondered if the murder weapon had been dropped somewhere inside. Similarly, Holmes continued to scan every inch of the ground as well as the tree trunk. The others watched him with interest.

"Here, look," Holmes indicated the ground, "That's the shoe mark of McCarthy who should've been pacing up and down for some time while he waited for his visitor. And this is his son, James' two-foot prints. One was that when he walked up to his father and the second one, bigger than the first, was when he had rushed to his father on hearing him scream. This endorses what he said was true. Now see the mysterious shoe marks here which show only the front half of the shoes. In other words, the man must be tip toeing towards McCarthy so as not to alert him with the intention of killing him. This shoe mark is square, a special shoe worn by cripples."

Holmes followed the shoe mark and found that the intruder must have come from the other side. He also collected some dust and waste from the ground there before he located a big stone behind the tree trunk. He spread a hanky over it and carried it. Placing it among the other collections, he went farther inside the wood and saw the main road that connects the woodland. Going back, he looked around, saw the lodge and excused himself saying that he would like to have a word with Moran there.

Minutes later, he returned. Then they all proceeded to their rooms. Holmes turned to Lestrade, indicating the big stone. "Preserve it, will you? It's the murder weapon. We need it to establish the facts." Lestrade who took a closer look at it, pointed out that there was no blood stain on it. "Yet this is the murder weapon," Holmes replied stubbornly.

"If so, who committed this murder?"

"Well, it's a left hander, tall but a cripple whose right leg is not in order. But he wears heavy-soled shoes, must be smoking

Indian cigars and carries knife, I mean a pen knife. There are more to it, but for the time being this'll do. It's my tips off to you. Mind you, hundreds of criminals may escape but not even one innocent be punished. Please work on your own. It's your baby now. Let me go back to my room."

"You mean, you no longer wish to probe the case?" Lestrade put in with an edge in his voice. Holmes turned and regarded him. "As far as I'm concerned, the case is solved. The assailant, as I told you a short while ago, is that man. It's a tough task to trace the offender from the description I gave you, but not impossible." With that they parted. Holmes and Dr Watson returned to the hotel in time for dinner. After dinner Holmes lit his pipe and analysed the case. "Two things put James in the clear. His father's saying something about *Rat* before he died remains unsolved. Next, his shouting as 'cooee.' He didn't know that his son James had returned from Bristol. So, as I told you before, it was a signal to the man whom he was to meet near the pool."

"This shouting 'cooee' – doesn't it look odd?" Dr Watson raised his doubt. "Well, it's common in Australia. So I heard. If so, it adds to the fact that the one Mc Carthy was to meet there must knows this Australian way of calling or an Australian-return!"

"Sounds convincing. But how about the word *Rat*?" Holmes did not answer at once. He took from his pocket a folded paper, straightened it as he extended it to Dr Watson, "It's the map of Victoria's colony. I gave a cable gram to a contact of mine in Australia. Just fold it here and see," he demonstrated, "It now reads 'ARAT.'

"Now remove the folding and read. It shows 'BALLART.' This Ballart is a place in Australia. His dying father had uttered this word ' ...RAT' to James to convey that the murderer was from Ballart. But James who was so stunned, didn't fully understand. He vaguely remembered that his father had said, 'A RAT.'

Dr Watson sat wonderstruck when Holmes continued, "By piecing another information that James had seen a grey coat near the scene of crime, it now adds up that the killer from Australia wore grey-coloured coat. Right? Now going meticulously, you've seen that the only access to the pool is either from the farm house or from Turner's estate. The killer's height and personality can be judged from the foot prints. That's what I'd observed and could give the detailed description of the killer. However, while studying deeply I found that the right shoe impression was very light while the left was heavy. So I said that his right leg wasn't in order."

"Looks true to me. In fact, though I was there on the scene I didn't notice so deeply.

By the way, what makes you say that he was a left hander?"

"From the nature of the wound. See, McCarthy was attacked behind his head. It was a severe blow that unless the assailant was a left hander and that too he was hiding behind the tree trunk when the father and son were quarreling, and finally slammed the stone down on the head of the victim after James had gone away.

And another thing about his smoking Indian cigars, I saw the ash and the cigar butt also. About the ash you're aware that

I had collected and experimented about 140 different kinds of tobaccos and their ashes from cigarette, pipes, cigars, etc.

They help me immensely in all my investigations. Hence I could tell now that in this case the assailant smoked Indian cigars. This particular butt was rolled thus in Rotterdam. Moreover, he had used a pipe because the end wasn't wet. And why I said that he had carried a pen knife which was blunt, because the cigar end was not bitten but cut irregular."

"I wonder who was the assailant who could do it so well. Who McCarthy had associated with in Australia......,"dragged Dr Watson.

"John Turner!" suddenly there came a voice as two men appeared in the doorway. One was the hotel waiter who brought in a stranger. It was the waiter who uttered John Turner's name. The stranger was a bit old and despite his well-built feature, he looked as if he was suffering with some prolonging illness. Holmes invited him in and indicated the sofa. "I saw your note routed through the waiter. Why you want to see me Mr Holmes?"

"It's about Mr McCarthy's tragic end. I know all about it. So I called you."

The stranger looked down at his palm as he spoke up, "I hate young James getting into trouble. I would've made a statement myself if it's not for my daughter! If she comes to know that I was behind it and you arrested me for this offence, nothing on the earth can console her!" Holmes shook his head. "I'm not the cop to arrest you. It's at the behest of your daughter I probed the case. However, I feel James must be released."

Turner cut a sorry figure as he said, "I'm already on the verge of death, Mr Holmes. With this diabetes keeps killing me each passing hour, I'd rather be house arrested than serving my sentence in the jail. Can you do something about it?" Holmes thought for a while before he produced a paper and pen, "Speak the truth Mr Turner. Let me jot down your true confession. But mind you, I intend to use it only when absolutely necessary. Okay?"

Turner's lips twisted with a dry smile as he divulged, "Well, Mr Holmes, to start with, what do you think my profession was?"

"Tell me," smiled Holmes. Turner glanced at Dr Watson. Knowing the sign Holmes told him about Dr Watson.

"I was a gangster in Australia," said Turner pausing. On hearing it Dr Watson reared back while it made no impact on Holmes.

"McCarthy was an accomplice. Yet he has made my life so miserable. For more than two decades, he was squeezing my blood. I was a care free young man, with six men, leading a shady life, robbing, waylaying and indulging in all underworld activities. The name of our gang is still known as Ballarat Gang and I, as Black Jack of Ballarat! One day we had intercepted a gold- laden wagon going from Ballarat to Melbourne. There were six men on board. In the encounter that ensued three of our men got knocked off. It so happened that McCarthy was the wagon driver. I had him cornered and was pointing a gun at him. He remained quiet, may be studying my features. I spared him, then my two gang members and I decamped with the booty of gold. We shared between us. I came back to England and settled down.

"I got married. But my wife died young leaving our tiny tot Alice, my only daughter.

For her sake, I shed all my shady activities and procured some estate and led a comfortable life. One day I ran into McCarthy in Regent Street. He remembered me all right. He nearly pleaded to accommodate him and his only son, however, blackmailing me that there's always a cop within earshot. He made such a fine bargain between black mailing and begging! I showed mercy and let him have my farmhouse free of cost.

That was the beginning of his pestering me. He kept squeezing for money and valuables. And he had got what he wanted."

Turner paused to gain some breath then continued, "But when he asked for Alice for James, I got annoyed. I was already an old man and that after my death he and his son could grab my wealth. This one thing I couldn't tolerate.

I refused. He threatened me. Yet I wouldn't budge. Then it was he who suggested that we talked this things over and invited me to the Boscombe pool that afternoon.

I lurked behind a tree and waited smoking when his son James arrived there.

"McCarthy urged his son to marry my daughter. I couldn't digest him becoming an heir to my property and own my daughter. There seemed no other way except to silence him! So I had to kill him. I've no regrets now. I'd do it over and again if it warrants. After that heavy blow he screamed and collapsed. James rushed to him. I thought of fleeing but only then I noticed my grey-coloured cloak that had fallen away. I hid behind the tree trunk and waited. The moment James turned his back to me, I went tip toeing and grabbed my cloak and bolted. That's all there's to it, Mr Holmes." With that he signed the statement and the witness signature was put by Dr Watson.

"Thanks Mr Turner. As I told you, I won't betray you unless James is proved innocent. You can take my words."

"Let this situation not come to anyone," muttered Turner as he got up then he staggered out. Holmes preserved the statement copy carefully, watching the court proceedings. In the mean time, he raised some doubts as and when the coroner or the police lawyer tried to pin James for the murder. Thus, Holmes was putting his best efforts to defend both James as well as Turner.

Finally, the benefit of doubt went in favour of James. He was released.

However, Turner did not live long. He died seven months later.

Alice and James got married. With the property they inherited they lived luxuriously.

According to Holmes, it was one hell of a case.

The Gloria Scott

It was a cold winter evening. With no immediate piece of work to attend to, Sherlock Holmes and Dr Watson were basking themselves before the hearth, smoking pipes.

"It's always the *first* in anything that goes down one's memory lane," spoke up the doctor. "My first case as a doctor in the army was an injured soldier, shot through the ankle. My hands were nearly shaking when I operated him. How about yours, my friend? What was your first case and how did you solve it?"

"Nice topic for the present moment. You can jot it down in your collection file," answered Holmes as he extracted an old, rusty cylinder, hardly a foot long, and forking his fingers he pulled out some rolled-up papers and straightened them.

"Here it is," Holmes addressed, "These are the killer papers that rattled Mr Trevor senior, Justice of peace and resulted in his sudden death." Dr Watson took the papers and read the contents. It read, "*The supply of game for London is steadily growing up. Head keeper, Hudson, has now been told to receive all orders for fly paper and for the preservation of your hen-pheasant's life!*"

"Looks odd, doesn't it? The content is as confusing as it appears strange. Just what it denotes? Is it a coded message?" asked Dr Watson.

"Well," Holmes went on, "Before I tell you what it's all about, I guess, I've to tell you something that mattered much. You know I seldom mix with people. It's sparring and fencing that occupy my outside world. While so, I struck acquaintance with one Mr Victor Trevor. I was taking a stroll in the street when Victor's dog had bitten me. I had to spend about 10 days in the hospital as an inpatient. During that time, Victor visited me in the hospital every day. It strengthened our friendship.

"After I had recuperated, I visited his place in Donnethorpe to stay for about a month. It was a nice place. Victor was looking after me very well. He introduced me to his father, Trevor senior. I got along well with them both. When I said I was a private eye, his father thought that I was blowing my own trumpet. He put a feeler to fathom my expertise. He told me to study him and tell him my observation about him. It was like a veritable challenge to me. But then that was part of my profession.

"I could see he was well built, yet he always carried a walking stick, his eyes were restless and although he wore a full-sleeved shirt he had rolled up the sleeves. Thus, after I took a quick, sweeping glance at him, I said that he constantly felt like a wolf in a trap. His restless eyes betrayed his fear for someone and hence he had made out a special walking stick which had been drilled and filled with molten lead the way many do. This is obviously to hit back when cornered. Soon after I said this, his smile slipped and he stiffened."

He agreed saying that some time back, they had intercepted a gang of poachers and handed them over to the authorities and since then the gang had been nursing a grudge against them and hence he was carrying the walking stick in self-defence.

"I added that boxing was his favourite sport as his flattened ears denoted that. He let that one drift, smiling. I then told him that he was digging for gold when he was young and that he had been to Japan and New Zealand. Finally, when I told him that he was a close associate of someone called J.A. and yet after some time he didn't get along well with that person, he sat stunned. Soon after I told that he passed out.

"Victor and I sprinkled some water on his face. Seconds later, he came to surface and apologised for causing us anxiety. He was all in praise for me for my power of observation. "But, how did you find out about J. A.?" he asked. "Oh, that was a simple thing to guess. I saw you have tattooed that initial J.A. on your forearm when you have rolled up your shirt sleeve, but then you have made an attempt to erase them later. Hence I told you about J.A."

Dr Watson nodded his head, grinning, mentally praising Holmes' efficiency.

"After that he became wordless. One evening when we were sitting in the lawn, the domestic help came and told him that he had a visitor. He was a short man, his dress was dirty and he looked weather beaten. The smell of brandy was advancing before him. I guessed he must be a sailor. Trevor asked him who he was and what he wanted, as if he was addressing a stranger. The visitor was not fooled by the cool manners of Trevor. He sounded surprised that Trevor did not recognize him. Then Trevor asked him if he was Hudson. He said, yes. "It's almost 30 years since we met.

I want to rest here for few days . Is it okay with you, or otherwise let me try with Mr Beddoes?" he had asked. Trevor got to his feet, muttered something and indicated the kitchen, saying that the domestic help would cater to his needs.

"I didn't pay much attention to what was going on there. The next morning I caught the return train back to London and was busy since then. After about a month I received a wire from Victor asking me to rush as he needed my help very badly. I obliged. Victor came to station to pick me up. On our way home he went on to say that things became worse after Hudson, the sailor, took refugee with them."

Said Victor, "My father, first, told him to work as a gardener. Days later, he wanted to be inducted as a butler and my father agreed. He seemed to have my father over a barrel for the reason best known to them. But my father never confided anything to me. As a butler, he began dominating the other servants. Instead of keeping Hudson under control, my father had to hike the salary of the other servants to retain them. He began waging his tail with my father, too. It irked me and I shoved him out of the kitchen one day."

Victor paused to look at Holmes and the doctor before he continued, "The next day Hudson packed up and told my father that he was leaving. My father apologised to him and asked me to tender an apology too. But I refused. Hudson left, saying that he would be looked after better at Beddoes' place. My father glared at me for some time, then said that I did not realise the consequences and that he'd tell me what it was all about when the time came. I let that one drift. However, I could see my father was upset as he confined himself most of the time in his study room, writing letters."

Holmes and Dr Watson sat quiet, listening to Victor's narration .

Victor added that a few days later a letter arrived from Hampshire in Fordingham. It had the impact of a thunderbolt. It played havoc with his father's life. He fainted after reading it, breathing heavily, his shirt front soaked with sweat. Surely it was a heart attack. He was rushed to the hospital. On regaining consciousness he found himself a paralysis. From then on, he remained as an in-patient in the hospital. According to the doctors he would not survive long. That's all there was to it. Seconds later, the coach entered into the street.

They saw a small crowd in front of the house. It endorsed that Mr Trevor was no more. A grief stricken Victor stormed inside and found his father was laid on a bench, his eyes half open with a fixed stare of death! Minutes later, on enquiry, the doctor said that his father died soon after he (Victor) had left for the station. "Before he died he had gained consciousness for a few seconds and told us that he had kept some important papers in the Japanese cabinet for you to see."

As there was nothing for Holmes to do, he remained in the study room brooding over about the letter which came from Hampshire. Suddenly, his eyes narrowed.

'Could it be that it was written by Hudson? If so, he (Hudson) must be in Hampshire where Beddoes lived. Or else, was it a tip off from Beddoes whom Hudson was blackmailing, too? Pleased with his hunch work, Holmes waited for Victor who came after some time and slipped the letter to Holmes. Holmes recollected the previous letter that read: *"The supply of game for London is steadily growing up. Head keeper Hudson, we believe, has now been told to receive all orders from fly paper and for the preservation of your pheasant's life."*

After hours of work, Holmes decoded the message. It was to read every third word in the sentence. It was a sort of caution. Accordingly, here it read, thus: *"The game is up! Hudson has told all. Fly for your life!"* When Holmes told this to Victor, he nodded saying that he had already found out that and showed the letter his dead father had kept for him in the Japanese cabinet.

"Dearest Son, Vic: Do not amiss my withholding the truth all these days. And do not have a scornful opinion about me after reading this true confession. The time has come now for me to divulge the whole episode. My actual name's James Armitage and not Trevor! I was a bank official. While serving in the London branch office about 30 years ago, I'd misappropriated the funds, hoping that I could make up soon after I got money.

But it didn't work out the way I'd figured. Despite my efforts to erase the tattoo mark J.A. on my forearm and change my name as Trevor, the long arm of the law nabbed me and I was shunted to Australia along with 37 other criminals on board the ship called, *The Gloria Scot!"*

The letter further said that convicts in each cell on board the ship had a criminal background, especially with white-collar crimes. While sailing in the boat, the convict at the adjacent cell called Jack Prendergast, a well-known fraudster in England accosted Trevor saying that he and some others were planning to revolt against the authorities and take possession of the ship, and asked Trevor if he would join hands with them. When Trevor pointed out that there were armed guards, Jack pacified that he had some inside help and there was nothing to worry. Jack also suggested Trevor to talk to the other convict in the next cell by name Evans, who was a master forger. Evans agreed on the spur of the moment.

"The chaplain on board the ship was hand in glove with these convicts," Trevor's letter went on, "He slipped each one a gun. It so happened that one day one of the convicts took ill and the doctor was summoned. While examining the patient the doctor spotted the hidden gun and raised an alarm. At once the other convicts pounced on him. They tied and gagged him, then bolted out through the open door way. The escaped convicts went on a shooting spree. They had shot down the skipper, guards and the entire crew. Now, we convicts took control of the ship. We all met at the deck and decided to abandon the ship and take a life boat. Only a few on board like the doctor and warders were spared. But Jack didn't want to leave any stone unturned. "I don't want to spare anybody to give an eyewitness account thereafter," he said. He gave us a compass, a barrel of water, chart and some snacks and bade us goodbye, advising us to say that we were shipwrecked if we ran into any ship."

The letter added that the escaped convicts referred to the chart to figure out in which direction they should proceed. The nearest land, Cape Verdes, was about 500 miles in the north. And Africa was 700 miles east. Trevor who had some marine knowledge found that the wind was blowing from north and hence suggested to head for Sierra Leone. While they were discussing this, suddenly they heard a loud bang. What they saw was a terrifying sight. It was their ship that exploded. A wall of orange coloured dancing flames shot up skywards, emitting a cloud of swirling black smoke.

"We made a U turn and headed fast to the burning ship," Trevor's letter continued, "Amidst the burning debris we saw a man clinging to a wooden plank. We rowed towards him. Someone whispered that his name was Hudson. He was badly hurt. He passed out after we hauled him up. However, when he surfaced the next morning, he told us that Jack and few other convicts who stayed overboard, wiped out the doctor and the warders too. But there was one who hit back. Sensing the trouble, that man had rushed to the arsenal and sat there before the gun powder with a match box, saying that if they dared to harm him he'd trigger the explosives and blow up the entire ship! Jack who wondered whether it was a real threat or just a hoax didn't know what to do. Then what followed no one knew. Suddenly, there was a deafening bang as the ship exploded, killing all on board, including Jack."

According to Trevor's letter, they were rescued by a passing ship. Trevor and Evans had changed their names, and like thousands of others who dig for gold, these two got lost with the pouring crowd and later returned at London and remained under cover with false names, until Hudson descended on the scene and unearthed the bitter past that, if leaked, would send Evans and Trevor to jail with triple life sentence. In the concluding lines, Trevor apologised to Victor for hiding these secrets all these years.

Sherlock Homes who narrated the first case of his to Dr Watson, went to the table and took some water, then lighting his pipe he joined his friend. "In the Post Script of the letter, Beddoes wrote to Trevor in coded language, as usual, that now they were wide open after Hudson's arrival and only God could save them. Reading between the lines, I can guess how Beddoes felt uneasy about Hudson's emergence," pointed out Homes.

"Naturally," nodded Dr Watson.

"Anyway," went on Holmes, "My client Victor wrote to me that he's well settled with his tea plantations and leading a peaceful life. As far as Beddoes and Hudson are concerned, no one knew anything about the duo. The police have a hunch that Hudson had wiped out Beddoes and is ducking out of sight. At the same time, they did not rule out that Beddoes could have killed Hudson and fled the country with all the money! That's all there's to it, my friend. Now you have been told the whole episode. You can have this case in your collection of files!"

"That's how the criminals crumble, don't they?" asked Dr Watson.

"Rightly said," replied Holmes.

The Crooked Man

It was close to midnight. Dr Watson emptied his pipe and was about to retire for bed when the front-door bell rang. He glanced at the grandfather clock and wondered who it was who wanted to see him at this hour of time.

After he had got married, he seldom found time to spend with his detective friend Sherlock Holmes. And knowing this, Holmes also did not wish to disturb him. Now could it be Holmes or someone who needed his urgent medical attention?

He went to the front door and opened it. Standing at the threshold was Sherlock Holmes. "What a surprise! Sleuth Sherlock Holmes finds time to visit his friend." beamed Dr Watson as he welcomed Holmes and took him inside. After exchanging the pleasantries, Homes said, "Hope I'm not disturbing you, Watson."

"Not at all. That you want to see me at this hour denotes that you're on to something very hot. Tell me, what do you want me to do?"

"You're very understanding, my friend. So long as we both have been sharing the same room, my investigation work went on smoothly with you assisting me. Now, after your marriage, I'm deprived of your company," spoke up Holmes.

"I'm always ready to help you. Tell me what do you want me to do?"

"A tricky case has come up. On the face of it, it appears to be a murder. But certain things lead me to think otherwise. I just can't figure it out as yet. I've to meet a person tomorrow at Aldershot. I want to take you with me."

"What's the case?" asked Dr Watson.

Now it was Holmes' turn to glance at the wall clock as he said, "Look, it's already midnight. Don't you feel sleepy?"

"No. Not after I've met you."

"Well, it has come out in the papers also," Holmes went on as he sat down and took out his pipe which he lit before he spoke up, "It's the mysterious death of Col Barclay of Aldershot. He was attached to the Regiment of the British Army, the Royal Munsters. It was camped at Aldershot. But Col Barclay was living in his bungalow, about a little distance away from the camp. It was he who commanded the Royal Munsters."

Holmes paused to smoke and added, "Needless to say that Col Barclay was a great soldier. That he had been quickly elevated to this level from an ordinary soldier, endorses it. He had married Ms Nancy Devoy, the daughter of a Sergeant. The couple had no issues. But that never bothered him. He was very fond of his wife. But, I heard it on the grapevine that his wife did not reciprocate his love for her. However, there was no dispute between them. This I learned from the coachman and a couple of servant maids who worked there for long."

Holmes puffed at his pipe before he continued, "The Col and his wife never went out together, but his wife did. She attended the church meetings occasionally. Whenever she did, she was accompanied by a neighbouring friend of her, by name Mrs Morrison. The meeting that commenced at 8 p.m. went on for an hour or so. It never varied during the last several months. The servant maids said so.

"But last week, it took a nasty turn. On reaching home from the church, Mrs Nancy Barclay went to the room on the west side partitioned by glass. It's the morning room. She asked the servant maid to fetch a cup of tea. Wondering, the maid prepared some tea and gave her. Meanwhile, the Col joined his wife. They sat talking. Suddenly their voices rose to top notch as they argued about something.

The servant maid went up and tried the door handle. But it was bolted from inside."

"She got rattled and brought the other maid and the coachman. Together they tried, but the door would not open. Inside, the Col and his wife were still arguing in high-pitched voice. Mrs Nancy shouted at him, "Coward! Give me back my life, you coward!" Then they heard the Col scream. The next moment, they heard a thud of someone falling down. With that the room plunged into silent."

"The bewildered servants didn't know what to do. But the coachman who knew the geography of the house, ran out and tried the windows. He found one of them open. He jumped in and rushed to the morning room. There he saw his employers: Col Barclay lay dead in a pool of blood from a deep cut mark on the head and Mrs Nancy was lying motionless, fainted. He searched for the keys, but couldn't find them. However, he called the police who summoned a carpenter and removed the door's bolt and went in."

Holmes, who found that his pipe had gone dead, relit it and spoke up, "The bungalow was swarmed with police and army. Then a colleague of Col Barclay, called Major Murphy, had sent for me and requested me to probe the case. On examining,

I found the dead Colonel's face appeared frightened. Either, he must've seen the attacker or realised that death was closing in on him. His eyes were wide open, obviously scared. And the key to the room was not to be seen anywhere! First, I spoke to Mrs Morrison. It got me nowhere. Then I grilled the three, the coachman and the two domestic help. It's only their statement that I've narrated to you so far. Then I probed further. After some time, one of them recollected that while arguing, Mrs Nancy had uttered the name, David!...."

"David? Why, it could be the surname of the deceased Colonel," voiced Dr Watson.

"No. The Colonel's first name is James," corrected Holmes. "Mrs Nancy was admitted in the hospital and the Colonel's body was sent for autopsy."

"It seems to be an open and shut case, doesn't it? Mrs Nancy had murdered her husband, hidden the key somewhere and faked a faint," pointed out Dr Watson.

"No, Watson. It's not so. I turned the room inside out. The key couldn't be located.

And another interesting feature is that, I found the footprints of a man outside the window. This morning room had a collection of antique weapons hung on the wall. There were swords, knives, shields, daggers, clubs, etc. Near the prostrate body was a heavy club! It's apparent that the offender must've scaled the compound wall and was hiding in the garden, before he sneaked in, grabbed the club from the row of antique weapons and murdered Col Barclay. On seeing it, Mrs Nancy had passed out. Meanwhile, the murderer saw the door being tried and so he had taken the key with him and escaped through the way he'd come."

"That's one theory. Another fact is that, I noticed the pug mark of an animal on the ground as well as over the window curtain," so saying Holmes extracted a paper from his pocket and straightened it. "This I've lifted from the ground outside the window. What this animal is and why the killer had brought it with him remains a puzzle! I turned every scrap of information in my mind. It then occurred to me that I should read between the lines. Why did Mrs Nancy ask for tea after returning from the church meeting at 9.15 p.m. unless something had happened to her there at the meeting or *en route* that kept bothering her?"

"I, once again, called on Mrs Morrison and asked her. After some persuasion she told me that on that night while they were returning home after the meeting at the church, there was a man who intercepted Mrs Nancy at the Hudson Street which was practically deserted then. This man was a bit aged, wearing the rags and looked crooked. On seeing Mrs Nancy he exclaimed, "Oh, Nancy, my god! Is that you, my dear?" It had rattled Mrs Nancy. Mrs Nancy uttered, "Henry, what a surprise! I thought you had died about 30 years ago! She then excused herself, took the crooked man aside and spoke to him for a while. They were talking in undertones. So, Mrs Morrison couldn't hear what they were talking about. However, when Mrs Nancy took leave from that man, he showed his fist at her threateningly and she was a bit annoyed."

"Why did Mrs Morrison not tell you this valuable information when first you questioned her?" Dr Watson put in.

"That's because Mrs Nancy had requested her not to tell anyone about it all. So, she didn't tell me."

"So, what's your next move?"

"I've enquired around about the crooked man at Alderstreet. He has rented a small portion in a house at Hudson Street. I spoke to the landlady. She told me that his name is Henry Wood, shifted to there hardly a week before and lived on performing magic during nights at the street corner and earned his bread. When I asked about the animal, she said he had carried something in a small box, but never saw what it contained. The landlady also exhibited a coin he had given to her for rent. They call it as a rupee in India. This crooked man was not at home when I went there. He's our only source of further probe. And I want to meet him tomorrow. If you accompany me, I'll be glad."

"Supposing he had quit the place in the mean time?"

"I've deployed a boy to have him watched and tail him wherever he goes. So, that won't be a problem."

"Come to think of it, you've nearly cracked the case, haven't you? Yet, what's the use of my coming with you?"

"To be my witness, as usual, when this conjurer makes a true confession to me. Besides, with you around, I can work peacefully. That is it."

The next morning Holmes and Dr Watson took the morning train and reached Alderstreet around 10. There the young boy hired by Holmes told them that the crooked man was in the house. Slipping a coin Holmes thanked the boy, then he and the doctor went to the house. Holmes sent his card across. Seconds later, the two stormed inside.

"Who are you and what do you want?" snapped the crooked man.

"Relax, Mr Henry Wood. I'm detective Sherlock Holmes, probing the murder of Col. Barclay and he's my friend, Dr Watson. We want to talk to you."

"What Braclay's death has to do with me?"

"Plenty. You're the last person who saw the Colonel alive! And your entry became his exit." said Holmes.

"No," the crooked man denied. "You can't implicate me. I've nothing to do with that."

"Well, if that's the way you feel, the murder rap will fall on Mrs Nancy." Holmes who knew the crooked man's soft corner for Mrs Nancy, hit him where it hurts.

The reaction of the crooked man was instantaneous. "No, Nancy wouldn't do a thing like that. She wouldn't ...."

"Hurt a fly!" interposed Holmes. "Is that what you're going to say? Listen, she's the obvious suspect. The servants heard her argue with her husband, then he fell dead with a fatal wound. That supplies a motive for her to wipe him out," kidded Holmes.

The crooked Henry Wood stared at Holmes for some time before he said, "Did you come to say just that?"

"You learn fast, Henry," smiled Holmes.

"What exactly do you want from me?" budged he.

"Go ahead and speak up. What happened on that night?" persisted Holmes.

"Well, it's a long story. It all began about 30 years ago when I was serving as a Corporal in the defence and Barclay was the sergeant. I was a handsome guy, then. I loved Nancy and she reciprocated my love. But her father had something else in his mind. He chose Barclay as his son-in-law. At that time our regiment was stationed in Bhurtee, a place in India. Suddenly, we found that the rebellions network was fast closing in on us. And our ration was depleting too. I wanted to alert our chief, General Neil, and seek his help. But I didn't want to run into our enemy. But, Barclay who knew the place like the back of his hand, offered to help me. He gave a freehand sketch of the secret route and that night after 10, I had secretly left."

"Until then, I never knew that Barclay was nursing a grudge against me because Nancy and I loved each other. His idea was to get rid of me and marry Nancy. So, he somehow betrayed my movement to the enemies! I was caught and held as a prisoner by the rebels who kept torturing me for years together. Then I was taken to Nepal where I spent months in fetter. One day the tribes there raided the camp, killed the rebels and took me with them to be their slave in the plantations. After some time I escaped from there and did some job, saved enough money and returned to England. This native place of mine gives me peace although I kept aloof from others, because no one will want to mingle with a crooked man like me."

"What happened then? I mean, after you've met Mrs Nancy accidentally on that night? You followed her, didn't you?"

"Do I've to say all that Mr Holmes? You seem to be knowing all," said Henry with a tinge of hurt in the voice.

"You followed her, hid in the garden, heard them quarrel and slipped inside through the window. How did Col Barclay react on seeing you?"

"He felt as if he was struck by a lightning," went on Henry. "His face went pale and eyes rolled back as he collapsed on the floor. His head hit the club and that resulted in a deep cut on the head from which blood was oozing out. I knew at the rate he was bleeding he wouldn't survive. However, I grabbed the key from Mrs Nancy and made an attempt to open the door and get help to shift him to the hospital. But a second thought stopped me. If I opened the door, I'd get caught for murdering Barclay. So, I pocketed the key and turned to go, but my Teddy stalled me a little..."

"Who's Teddy? Is that the animal you carry with you?" asked Holmes.

"Yes. He's a mongoose! He's my meal ticket! I use him in all my magic show. Teddy saw a canary above and tried to catch it by climbing up the window curtain. It took some time for me to get hold of him, put him in the box and bolt! That's the whole episode Mr Holmes. Neither Nancy nor I killed Barclay. It was an accidental death. A freak accident."

Holmes shifted to a more comfortable position. He knew Henry spoke the truth.

However, he said cautiously that if there's an inquest, he (Henry) would be called for. "Till then I advise you not to leave the town. Is that understood?"

Once outside, Holmes and Dr Watson saw Major Murphy go. On seeing the duo, Murphy paused as he said, "Mr Holmes, have you heard the autopsy report? The doctor says that Col Barclay died of apoplexy! That puts Mrs Nancy in the clear."

Thanking the Major for the information, Holmes and Dr Watson took a coach and went back to the railway station to catch the next train back home.

"If that puts Mrs Nancy in the clear, it also puts the crooked man Henry Wood in the clear, doesn't it?" smiled Dr Watson.

"It puts even Teddy also in the clear." Holmes said and grinned.

"By the way, I forgot to ask you. Who's David? Why did Mrs Nancy utter that name when she argued with her husband?"

"O, you know she was a member of the church and had been attending all the meetings? So, it was the episode of David from the Bible she was quoting about Col Barclay's betrayal of Henry Wood."

As they entered into the platform, the Upper Quadrant Starter Signal at the station changed into green as if to announce the arrival of the train!

The Adventure of The Dancing Man

That morning Sherlock Holmes sat filling his pipe when Dr Watson breezed in.

"You, been busy?" he smiled.

"Yeah, busy doing nothing," Holmes returned the smile. As if waiting for this moment, Holmes slipped a full-scale paper to his friend. "See, what can you make of it?" asked he. Dr Watson opened it and saw a hand-drawn picture of a man dancing. "Looks like a childish stuff!" he answered keeping the paper on the table.

"It's a case shrouded with mystery. We'll know about it in a little while," said Holmes

Just then there came a tap on the door, then it swung open as a man stepped inside.

He was tall and proportionately built with a clean-shaven face. Holmes welcomed him saying that he had received his letter and told him to go into details so that Dr Watson could also hear it.

Mr Cubit, the visitor, nodded at Dr Watson before he narrated, "Well, Mr Holmes, prior to that I'm necessitated to tell you something. We were earlier living at Thorpe Manor for five centuries. Ours was a middle-class family, but with a high reputation and known across entire Norfolk. It so happened when I'd visited London last year, I stumbled onto my American wife, Elsie, in a restaurant in Russel Square. It was an instant love, of course, and a month after that I had married her in a Registrar Office there and shifted to Norfolk.

"Elsie was a marvellous woman and we loved each other the way we do even now. She said that there were some persons whom she did not want to remember and that I was not to plunge into her past. I agreed spontaneously. Last week she got upset after receiving a letter from USA. She didn't even show it to me. She flung it in the fire place. A month after I spotted a picture of a Dancing Man, scribbled by someone. I thought our stable boy might've drawn it, but he said he didn't. I'd wiped it clean and casually mentioned it to my wife. It, indeed, jolted her. She wanted me to show if any more pictures appeared on the front door. And this paper I'd sent to you yesterday came in last Tuesday. When I had shown it to her, she passed out. I don't know why she's scared on seeing it. She didn't confide in me, nor did I want to break my promise. That's the dilemma. I want you to look into it."

Holmes took the paper near the window and held it at arm's length against the sun light. But there was no tell-tale clue on it. So he pacified Mr Cubit saying that if only he (Mr Cubit) had not destroyed the first letter, he could piece them together.

"It's a coded message. That's all I can tell you now Mr Cubit. If any more letters arrive, please bring them to me or post it. I'll try to dig some facts out of it. Okay?

Meanwhile, find out if possible, about any new comer to your area."

For the next two weeks Holmes did not hear from his client. Then he received a wire that Mr Cubit would be coming that morning. With his face grim Mr Cubit walked in. "Here comes a series of bolts out of blue," he sounded exhausted as he dropped some papers and sat heavily. "The first two were pasted on the door when I went back after meeting you. Another one was seen dropped two days later. And three days after that one more was pasted. I've brought all of them for your scrutiny. I'm terribly worried, Mr Holmes. Of late, my wife feels terribly sick. She twice attempted to tell me the truth, but changed her mind at last. And I didn't pester her."

"I've seen the man who draws the pictures," continued Mr Cubit, "The other day I sat unseen and kept a watchful eye at the gate, keeping my gun ready. My wife urged me to skip it. But I didn't want to. Sometime during the wee hours I saw a man come and pause before the gate and began writing. I quickly got up to nab him.

But my wife clung on to me, not allowing me to go out. The intruder must've heard the scuffle between us and by the time, I managed to free myself and rush out, he was gone! I couldn't figure why my wife had blocked me! However, when I went out in the morning, there it was, the same picture he'd drawn a couple of days ago. Here it is," he extended another paper.

Holmes took it. "Well, Mr Cubit," he spoke soothingly, "Leave it to me. I'll decode all these and call on you in due course of time." Nodding, Mr Cubit left. Holmes took the bunch of papers and examined them for a long time. Then his frown cleared as he seemed to have found out something. He wrote a brief cable gram, saying that if he could get an answer within two days, he would possibly be able to crack the case. But before he could get an answer to his query, he received a letter from Mr Cubit in which he had enclosed a copy of the message which he (Mr Cubit) found in his out-house.

The message electrified even Holmes. He and Dr Watson, at once, proceeded to North Walsham station. Soon after they reached their destination, the Station Master on duty there enquired whether they were the detectives from Baker Street. When Holmes nodded, the SM said, "I saw our area inspector Mr Martin go. I'm sorry to state gentlemen that Mr Cubit is dead and his wife is serious!"

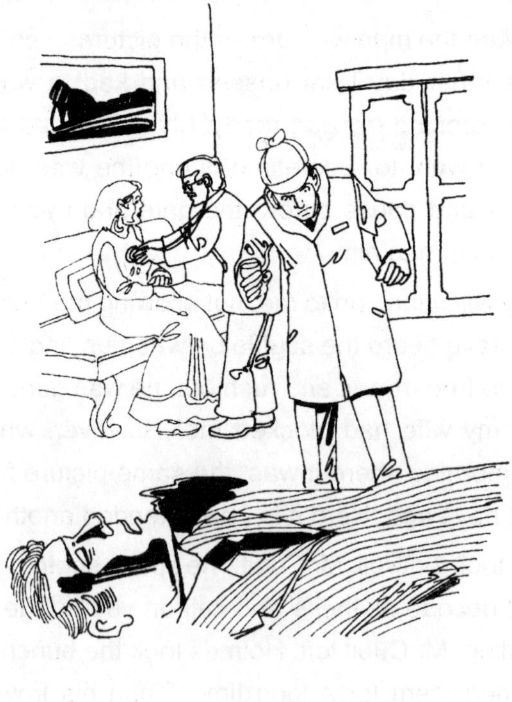

It rocked Holmes, because none of his clients had ever died half way through an investigation. At the house a big crowd had gathered. Inspector Martin welcomed the duo and took them inside the dimly lit study room where a candle was burning. Mr Cubit's body lay on the floor amidst a pool of blood swarmed with flies while his injured wife was propping up against the wall, gasping. An aged doctor was examining her.

"The lady is badly hurt by the bullet wound. Her survival is unpredictable. The cook and the servant maid had heard the gun shot, rushed to the study room and called us. Meanwhile, the killer had fled the scene." Holmes took a stroll, his eyes missing nothing. In the corridor he could still smell the gun powder. Then as ordered by Holmes, the two servant maids, Mrs Sanders and the cook Mrs King were brought. On enquiry they said, they were fast asleep when there came two gun shots, the second one sounded louder than the first one.

Holmes found that two shots were fired from Mr Cubit's gun. Martin concluded that Mr Cubit had shot his wife and then shot himself or the lady should've shot her husband and attempted to shoot herself. But Holmes' shrewd brain refused to accept his theory. Indicating the window panel where a bullet got stuck, Holmes voiced that someone was shooting from the corridor and that's why there's this smell of gun powder. "At that time the window was left open for a brief period, then it was shut. Hence, the candle didn't get extinguished! Come to think of this shooting, there should've been a gun battle between Mr Cubit and the intruder. While Mr Cubit's shot hit the window panel, the assailant's bullet killed Mr Cubit. And about his wounded wife, the second shot fired either by Mr Cubit or the one by the murderer must've hit her. However, the second round fired by Mr Cubit and the first by the intruder must've occurred simultaneously. That's why the cook said that the second bang was louder than the first one."

Holmes' observation made Martin gape after him. He never thought that Holmes would be so shrewd. Holmes saw a lady handbag on the table. He took the bag and opened it. Neatly stacked inside were 20 nos. of currencies in 50 pounds denomination. "It's your baby now," Holmes gave the bag to Martin. The probing men went out near the window. There they saw the footprints of a big man. Beside it, lay a bullet. "This leads to a showdown," Holmes said and moved inside followed by the others.

Once inside, Holmes asked them, "Did any of you know an inn somewhere here called Elrieg's. At once the stable boy stepped forward saying that he knew the location. "Elreige is a farmer, sir," he added. Holmes took out the last sheet of the Dancing Man picture, scrutinized it for some time before he scribbled a note and slipped it to the stable boy. "Hand this letter over to Mr Abe Slanley, in person and not to anybody else," he cautioned.

After the boy had left, Holmes beckoned to Dr Watson and Martin near him and took out the bunch of Dancing Man's pictures and spread them on the table. Tapping the sheets, Holmes narrated what he had observed in the investigation so far. "The assailant is called Abe Slanley, the addressee of my letter. It may be surprising to you as to how I've figured it out. Well, the key to the mystery is this: you see, vowel 'E' is widely used in English language. Of the 15 messages I came across, it appears four times. At the same time, decoding any other letter like, A, D, H, I, N, O, R, S, T will be a futile attempt and also a time-consuming process. When I get more sheets of messages, I kept the ball rolling. Another message with a single letter E as the second and the fourth letter made me to presume that it was a five- letter word with two Es present in the middle like LEVER or SEVER, or NEVER. Of these three words, NEVER seemed more true here for it answered to a question. Then came the other consonant NVR. So, it endorsed that the message was nothing but a reply, NEVER.

"Similarly, I kept at it non-stop and decoded more messages. One said that 'AM HERE.'- ABE SLANLEY. And another revealed, 'AT ELRIGES!' Now ask yourself the sixty-four –thousand –dollar –question. Who's this man called Abe Slanley? Why should he write such mysterious letters? To whom was he writing? One thing is clear. That he had pasted them on the door at Cubit's house meant he was hinting one of the inmates there. That rules out Mr Cubit. So, I'm forced to conclude that Mrs Cubit knows this man and vice versa. He must've told Mrs Cubit to call on him at Elriges. That's it. On seeing it, I contacted Wilson Hargreave of NYPD and learned that Abe Slanley was a deadly crook in Chicago."

"Later that evening another message I was given, which after I'd deciphered, read "ELSIE,_RE_ARE TO MEET THY GO_" After working at it, I learned that the decoded message meant, "ELSIE, PREPARE TO MEET THY GOD!" This message denoted that Abe Slanley was planning to eliminate them both. So, I dashed here with Dr Watson to stop this killing. But the killer was a shade quicker than me." Holmes lifted his hands up and dropped them in a helpless gesture.

Inspector Martin stirred, "I really appreciate you for your unparalleled probe. But I wonder why should we wait for the killer to walk in? Can't we rush there and nab him?"

"I've set a trap to pay him back in his own coin," went on Holmes, "When my coded message that reads, "*Come here at once,"* reaches him he'd immediately think that it was Mrs Cubit who wrote to him and he'd storm in a hurry. Just wait and see."

As predicted by Holmes, minutes later, a man burst in impatiently. He was tall, solidly built and rather handsome, wearing a well-tailored dress. But on seeing the two men,

Holmes and Martin, pointing guns at him he came to a standstill. At a nod from Holmes, Dr Watson moved to him and took out his gun while Martin slipped the handcuffs.

"I never thought that my dear Elsie would trap me like this and betray me to the police," he muttered.

"You're mistaken Abe. It was not Mrs Cubit. Right now she's fighting for her life after having been shot at last night," said Holmes.

"Do you think I'd believe that yarn? Who shot her? It wasn't me. And if not Elsie who wrote that coded message inviting me here?" he snapped. "Except for Elsie whom I'd taught it, no one here knows it. It's the secret language of our own outfit in America."

"I did it, Abe. In case you do not know about me, I'm Sherlock Holmes."

At the mention of the name Sherlock Holmes, such a dreaded gangster like Abe Slanley reared back spontaneously. He had heard a lot about Holmes and seen his photos too. But those photos were not very clear, showing only the side face.

"Abe, I want you to be sensible about it. Speak the truth or else, we'll be forced to close the case that Mrs Cubit had shot her husband," addressed Holmes meaningfully.

For a few seconds, Abe Slanley remained quiet, obviously, tortured by moral thought, then he said, "Don't try the kid, sir. I'm crazy about her. I've been in love with her right from our younger days. And she too reciprocated my love for her. Her father was the kingpin of our gang. It was he who invented this code language. And I worked for him. Knowing our love affair, her father offered his daughter's hand in marriage with me. She was engaged to me. But she insisted that unless I reformed myself, she wouldn't marry me. But by then I'd merged myself too deeply with the gang that I couldn't come out."

"One day she had eloped with an Englishman. But I traced her whereabouts and through the coded messages invited her to join me, but she wouldn't. She begged me to lay off her and her husband whose reputation would dent if she ran off with me. I felt sorry for her because I still love her so deeply. The other day she told me to come near the window at the small hours. I went. She opened the window and I stood talking with her. But when sh.. aid she'd offer me some money, I got mad and I very nearly pulled her out when her husband materialized. I took out my gun just to scare him away. But the fool had opened fire. Luckily, it didn't hit me. I fired back, hitting him squarely on the chest and ran away when I heard the window being shut after me. So I didn't shoot Elsie. Now when you tell me that she was shot at, I think either she got caught in the cross fire or her husband, suspecting her, must've shot her before he succumbed to the bullet wound. Since then I've been hiding in my place when this coded message invited me. Feeling thrilled that Elsie had written to me, I walked in and the rest you know," he shrugged in a helpless gesture.

Holmes nodded as he turned to Martin and told him to carry on with his work. Abe asked if he could see Elsie, but Martin told him that Mrs Cubit was still unconscious. "Save it," he said mockingly, "You can see her without any interruption after you've served the jail sentence and got released. Now move on," he went nudging Abe, waving to Holmes and Dr Watson.

Abe drew 20 years jail sentence for his crimes. Mrs Cubit underwent an operation and recuperated a few months later. Upon returning home, she just led her life in dreams of yesterday!

Elsewhere in Baker Street, Dr Watson was reading the newspaper about the whole episode and how Holmes had cracked the most toughest case.

Sherlock Holmes? He was busy doing nothing but filling his pipe!

The Adventure of The Abbey Grange

Abbey Grange
Marsham , KENT.
Time 3. 30 p.m.

"Dear Mr Holmes:

I would be very much obliged if you will intervene and help me solve a murder mystery. This seems to me to be a veritably challenging one. Now I'm under spot light, for the victim, Sir Eustace, was a popular rich man and hence the press is also closely watching my every move. I let go of the lady but cordoned off the scene of crime so that the clues whatever available will remain undisturbed. Please rush, will you?"

Thanking you
Yours truly

Hopkins
Inspector of Police

"If I remember all right, this's the seventh case that Hopkins gives an SOS call. I must say it's no exaggeration that he'd mentioned as veritably challenging one, because every case he referred to me so far have been really mind-boggling," remarked Holmes. Twenty minutes later, they were on board the train bound for Kent. From there a coach swiftly took them to the destination: a big house with a wrought iron gates.

Hopkins received them at the gate and took them inside. "Glad you've come," he accosted, "The victim, as I mentioned in my cable gram, Sir Eustace Brackenstall, was a very influential man. He draws lots of water here...."

"Whether rich or poor, once dead all are covered by the same moss," Commented Holmes as he didn't like Hopkins treating it in velvet glove. Hopkins, who understood the sign quickly, added, "It seems Mr Holmes that he was slain by the notorious gang—three Randals! He was hit by the poker. His mistress is in a terrible shock."

Holmes did not speak. He knew about the three Randals. They were, a father and his two sons, the dreaded decoits who wouldn't stop at nothing. Hopkins ushered them to the living room where Mrs Brackenstall sat on a chair, her head held in her hands. Hopkins spoke acidly, requesting her to narrate the whole episode to Holmes.

Despite her middle age, she was very pretty with provocative curves and blonde hairs. Her eyes gazed intently at the visitors. Then clearing her throat she spoke in a musical voice. "A little after 10 last night I sat reading a book. The lord was sleeping in his room upstairs. And our servants were in their quarters. When the wall clock struck 11, I kept the book aside and took a look around to see everything was intact. I mean, the doors and windows closed. With a candle I went near the dining room window and the French window behind it which stood open, but stopped short wordless at the sight of three men standing outside!"

Mrs Brackenstall further stated that one of them, a senior followed by two other young men, tried to enter inside. She opened her mouth to scream, but the first man sprang up, caught her by the neck and muffled her voice. Yet, she struggled. But a hard slap from that fellow finally put her out of conscious. When she surfaced, she found herself tied to the chair by the bell rope and gagged.

"It was at this moment the lord came down with a cudgel," continued Mrs Brackenstall, "Maybe he'd heard the noise. On seeing them he darted ahead to strike them with his cudgel. But his age and soft living were no match to them. One of them grabbed the poker from the fire place and hit him hard on the head that killed the lord instantaneously. I passed out on seeing my husband being slain. When I regained consciousness, they were still there, taking with them the silver article kept in the shelf besides helping themselves to a bottle of liquor from the cabinet."

Mrs Brackenstall added that the senior of the three was a bearded man and his two sons were clean shaven and each had a drink before they kept the empty wine glasses on the table and went out through the window they had come. For the next ten minutes or so after they had left, she tried to wriggle out before she managed to remove the cloth by which they had gagged her. The next moment her scream brought the servants to the scene. They freed her and called the police. Holmes noticed that the poker lying beside the corpse was slightly bent at one side, denoting that the blow was deadly.

Holmes examined the three wine glasses the three men had used and the bottle too. He found that the bottle was opened by a penknife's corkscrew. On sniffing each glass he found that only two glasses contained some wine while the third had been merely used as a waste collector.

"Did the lady see the three drink?" Holmes asked Hopkins.

"Yes, that's what she said. She saw them drink," replied Hopkins.

"I wonder why did they spare Mrs Brackenstall. After all she's the eyewitness in the case, doesn't she?"

"Yes," nodded Hopkins thoughtfully. "You see she was unconscious at that time, wasn't she?"

"All right, now I want to talk to the servants," Holmes announced. Seconds later, they were all sitting down in the living room opposite to Mrs Brackenstall. The servant maid was a middle-aged woman. She said that on hearing the scream she rushed to the dining room and untied her, then together they summoned for the police. When Holmes asked whether by chance she had seen the killers, the maid nodded, "Of course, sometime before this incident I saw three men near the gate. But I thought nothing of it, then."

"You said you saw three men near the gate at that time of hours. Didn't it occur to you that they could be the three Randals?"

"I told you, my mind was busy that I scarcely registered what I'd seen. It was just a glimpse." While they were talking,

Mrs Brackenstall's sleeve fell back, revealing the mark of a wound on her forearm. She quickly covered it, but not before Holmes had seen it. "I suppose that is the injury you sustained last night?" he enquired.

She shook her head and looked at Hopkins who acted as her mouthpiece and said that it was inflicted by the lord. "He's a gem of a man so long as he's sober, Mr Holmes. But the moment he hits the bottle, he becomes very wild. He'd once set her pet dog on fire, you know? Such was his temperament."

Mrs Brackenstall who remained silent until then spoke up, "Our neighbours here know what a horrible man he is under the influence of alcohol. Our servant quarters is away in the adjacent block and the maid Theresa's room was above ours. So none can hear what goes on here in the dining room or in our bedroom. Incidentally, Theresa has been with me right from my younger days. She knows how I've been suffering the strong-arm tactics of my husband."

"Can you show me where you were and where the three men stood before entering in?" Holmes insisted. She got up and led them to the well-furnished dining room, with a French window, apart from three smaller windows there. Indicating the chair, she said, "I was tied to this chair." Holmes saw the bell rope with which she had been tied was still there on the chair. Turning to Hopkins, he praised him, "You really took pains to keep every thing as-is condition." Hopkins smiled throwing a dogmatic look around and at Mrs Brackenstall.

"Where did they get this cord from?" asked Holmes.

"Oh, it's the bell cord which they had pulled from the window curtain," answered Hopkins. Holmes straightened up. "Well

Hopkins, it's your baby now. It, indeed, looks like the handiwork of the three Randals. I wish you good luck:" Holmes and Dr Watson shook hands with him, nodded at the others and left.

During their return journey *en route,* Holmes pulled Dr Watson's hand and hurriedly got down from the train. "I want them, including Hopkins, to think that I'd believed their yarn. Let me take another closer look and re-establish the facts, because the lord's wife had obviously lied to me saying that the three men had a drink. It wasn't so. I told you, only two glasses contained the wine and the third was used as a waste collector. Yet, she said she'd seen the three drink. I couldn't guess why she lied!"

They took a return train to Kent. In just under 15 minutes they reached the lord's house. Hopkins was not there. Holmes, followed by Dr Watson, went to the dining room where the former began his probe. His eyes went examining every inch of the floor, the wall and the chair, as also the knots on the rope. He saw the window from where the bell rope was pulled down. He stood erect and stretched his hand above to reach the bell rope top in vain. Then he observed that the window sill was slightly stained at one place. "The murderer must be a tall man. However, like me, he couldn't reach the bell rope. So he'd put one leg on the sill and so the thin layer of dust is present here."

"Another blunder by the lady is that, she said that the bell rope had been pulled down by them, didn't she? But it was never pulled down. It was cut about three inches from the top. Moreover, the chair she said she was tied to, had a drop of blood stain at one corner. Maybe you haven't seen that. This blood drop was obviously from the wound sustained by the lord. If the lady had been tied to the chair, how could this blood drop fall on the chair and not on her? What I'm driving at is, the lady was not tied to the seat when the lord was hit on the head. In other words, she had lied that she was tied to the chair. Not only she, the maid, Theresa, also lied that it was she who had untied her mistress. Do you follow me?"

Dr Watson who quickly turned the whole episode in his mind, nodded his head in agreement. "Naturally your observation points an accusing finger at the two women." Holmes then called the maid Theresa. "I learn that you were with the mistress for a long time. If the lord is a wild temperament man, he could've treated you, too roughly at one time or the other, couldn't he?"

Theresa said yes and added that once he had hurled a decanter at her which missed her by inches.

"Tell me when and where the lord had first met your mistress?"

"About 18 months back when we were coming to London by the ship."

"Can you tell me the name of ship and the exact date of your travel?"

"I don't remember. It's Gilbert or something. And I forgot the date of travel also. Maybe, the mistress remembers that."

"I take, it was while you were sailing in the ship to London that your mistress had struck an acquaintance with the lord?" Holmes slipped his trap question so casually in a bored voice.

No, not with the lord. It was the first officer in the ship called Jack Crocker whom she struck an acquaintance with. He spoke very kindly and was a big help to us throughout the voyage."

"I see, I thought the lord also travelled with you and they met on board the ship."

"No, no. The lord met her here in London, that's last June to be exact."

"Thank you, Mrs Theresa. You've been very *understanding* towards your mistress." Holmes who gave a stress to the word *understanding,* got to his feet and went in to meet Mrs Brackenstall. On seeing Holmes, her left eyebrow shot up quizzically, "Any more questions?" she sounded curt the way you would regard an arrogant hotel waiter.

"No more question, lady. It's your true confession that I want to hear."

"What do you mean, true confession?"

"Lady, dictionary defines *confession* as a formal statement that you've done something wrong. When you said about the three Randals, you didn't speak the truth to me."

"Are you trying to hook me in this murder case, Mr Holmes? Is it the way to treat a woman who lost her husband and nearly kissed her death?"

"Lady, in any homicide case, especially, when the wife gets knocked off the first suspect is her husband, and vice versa."

At this juncture, Theresa stormed in angrily and said. "Lay off my mistress, Mr Holmes. Your intervention is like rubbing salt to the wound."

Holmes smiled. "This is what I said minutes before. You're very *understanding* towards your mistress," so saying he left, followed by Dr Watson, leaving the two women staring after them and exchanging a glance.

When Holmes came out to the portico, he saw the pond that had frozen now due to the cold climate. He took out the scribbling pad from his coat pocket, wrote *"Dear Mr Hopkins, dredge the pond"*—Sherlock Holmes. He slipped the note to the lodge keeper with an instruction to forward it to inspector Hopkins. Then the duo proceeded to London.

Around 2 p.m. after the lunch in a restaurant, Holmes and Dr Watson went to a shipping company. Holmes gave his card at the reception and sat down. As if waiting for him, the manager himself came out and took the two inside with utmost respect. "I've read and heard a lot about you two, gentlemen. Please tell me what can I do for you. The pleasure is mine."

For the next ten minutes they sat talking, then left but not before Holmes learned that the name of the ship was *Rock Of Gibraltar* and that Miss Mary Fraser, now known as Mrs Brackenstall, sailed to London the previous year in 1895. They had retained the same crew member, including Jack Crocker, the then First Officer who recently got elevated to the rank of a captain and he would be commanding the new ship, *The Bass Rock.* He was a fine sea man, however, the only problem with Crocker was that he was too quick in doing things and seldom gave a second thought.

By the time Holmes and Dr Watson returned to Baker Street residence, inspector Hopkins was there, waiting impatiently. "I got your note and dredged the pond. Underneath I found the stolen silver articles. Another thing that adds mystery to it is that, the three Randals were arrested by New York police. If so, who murdered the lord here?"

"You'll know all that – I mean, 5 Ws and 1 How- in a day," Holmes assured.

"What 5 Ws and 1 H?"

"Who, what, when , why, where and How—all these questions related to the offender will be known in a day."

"The earlier it is solved, the better," Hopkins checked the interior of his hat, frowned, put it on and took leave.

After he had left, Holmes told Dr Watson, "We'll meet the killer in a little while."

Minutes later, a well-dressed tall and powerfully built, middle-aged man stepped in.

"I'm Skipper Crocker, Mr Holmes," he introduced to himself, "I got your note asking me to pay you a visit. Hence I'm here now."

"Please sit," Holmes indicated the vacant chair into which he lowered his weight.

"Smoke if you feel like," Holmes jerked his head at Dr Watson who gave him a cigar which Crocker lit up with unsteady hands.

"Glad you've been made the captain of the ship, *The Bass Rock,"* Holmes went on coolly, "You may wonder how I knew this. Not only this. I know what had happened last night and how Sir Eustace got knocked off and your involvement, too. So, do not hide anything from me. Play along and you won't regret it."

"Play along and you won't regret it!"

Such an encouragement from Holmes was like a catalyst to Crocker. He puffed at the cigar and began speaking. "Last year I met Miss Mary Fraser when she travelled in my ship *The Rock Of Gibraltar* and fell in love with her. But to my dismay she didn't reciprocate my love. As far as she was concerned I was just a good friend. That's all. During those few days when our ship was berthed at the harbour, I tried to meet her. But it failed. Meanwhile, our ship left London and set sail to far off places. Nearly one year elapsed. But my love for her didn't wither."

"This time when I reached London, I located her residence and went there last night and hung on near the window. When she came to the window and saw me, she surprisingly opened it wider and let me in. She was narrating her endless ordeal with her husband. Suddenly, he descended on the scene with a cudgel in hand, saw us both, then hit her, first, on the head before he jumped on me menacingly."

"It drove me crazy not because he attempted to hit me, but the way he had treated her in my presence. So, I frantically looked around, spotted the poker near the fire place and that was that. His skull broke and he succumbed to the injury. Meanwhile, on hearing the scream of Miss Fraser, Theresa rushed to the scene. It was she who helped Miss Fraser. In order to sober her up, she mixed a drink. Since there was nothing I could do, I left. Maybe, after the booze she returned to her normal self. Then we planned and cooked up a safe story that it was the three Randals." Crocker stubbed out the cigar.

"But you didn't tell me that you had cut the bell rope and tied her to the chair?"

"Sorry, sir. It's not intentional. I just forgot."

"See, no matter how careful one is, certain things betray one. In your case it's the knots on the chair. It was a special knot put only by the seamen like you."

Crocker said dryly, "The problem with me is that, I'm good at sea, but on land, as they say, I'm a hot head. I just take quick, hasty decision not realizing the outcome."

There was a pause then Crocker asked what would happen to him. "Well, I'd rather say that after seeing my findings in black & white, you may have a faint chance of beating the rap. But Mrs Brackenstall would be taken into task."

On hearing it, Crocker's face fell. "I can't bear the thought of her landing behind the bars, Mr Holmes. In that case, I'll submit myself to the police to free her."

Holmes regarded him for a few seconds, before he said, "I just tested your love for her. Anyway, let's try a mock court case now. Assume that I'm the judge, accusing you of the crime and let my friend Dr Watosn be the jury. What do you make of it, Watson?"

"I dare say, your honour that Mr Crocker is not guilty," opined Dr Watson.

"See, what our court of law says? It'd be concluded in the similar fashion at the real court too. Now skipper, you get off. Come back after a year or two if your love for the red head withstands the weather of time. Meanwhile, she will have served the sentence and be ready to accommodate you in her heart." Holmes meant what he said.

"So that makes you both two heads," commented Dr Watson, "You, the hot head and she, the red head! As they say two heads are better than one, isn't it?"

There was a thunderous laughter. Even Crocker also burst out laughing!

The Adventure of The Cardboard Box

"This sweltering heat is killing me," announced Dr Watson "That makes two of us, friend," shrugged Sherlock Holmes, the master detective.

"I envy the people who live in Croydon. It's rather cool and pleasant out there."

"Is it? I wonder why I shouldn't make your dream come true!"

Dr Watson glanced at him sharply, "You, kidding me?" he snapped. "Nope! Here, read this news," Holmes tapped a news item in the paper as he pushed the folded newspaper across the table. Dr Watson looked at it. Of course, there was an interesting piece of news. It read that one lady by name Miss Susan Cushing living at Cross Street in Croydon, had received a parcel by post the previous afternoon at 2 p.m. What was so odd about it was that, the cardboard box was full of powdered salt and in it were buried two human ears. Both the ears appeared to have been severed only recently with sticky blood clot on them!

It rattled the lady. She called the police. On arriving, the police squad, headed by Inspector Lestrade, examined it. The parcel was sent by post from Belfast. According to Miss

Susan, it could be the handiwork of the three medicos who had rented a portion of her house before. But as the days passed the students became nuisance and hence Miss Susan had to evict them all. Maybe, it had annoyed them and they sent this parcel to upset her. Moreover, as medical students their chances of acquiring such dissected human body parts during autopsy were more. And as if to point an accusing finger at them, Miss Susan remembered one of them was from Belfast. That was all the police could say. And the news concluded, as usual, that further probe was on. After Dr Watson had read the news, Holmes extended a small paper to him. It was a telegram from Inspector Lestrade, requesting them to come and help him in his investigation. "So that's it, my friend. Get ready," said Holmes. Dr Watson needed no further invitation. He immediately got to his feet.

The next morning Holmes gave a wire to Lestrade about their visit before he and Dr Watson caught the morning train and left for Croydon. It was drizzling when they arrived at the destination. They checked in a hotel, left their luggage and proceeded to Cross Street. They saw Inspector Lestrade waiting for them. The arrival of Sherlock Holmes renewed his confidence as he knew from the past experience that no matter how tricky a case be, Holmes would crack it soon.

Lestrade welcomed the duo and took them inside. Just then a lady, aged about 50, pleaded to Lestrade to remove the cardboard box. "The sight of it gives me jitters," she muttered, eyeing the other two. Lestrade assured that he would do that and introduced Holmes and Dr Watson to her.

Lestrade then took Holmes and showed the parcel. Holmes' eagle eyes scanned it. He, among other things, observed that the rectangular cardboard box was a half-pound honeydew box available at every nook and cranny. Inside, it was full of table salt. Holmes brushed aside the salt and took out from it two human ears with a tong, examined them at close quarters before placing them on the nearby table.

Moments later, he called Lestrade and said, "The two ears are not pairs. I mean, they did not belong to one person. The one with a punctured mark on it, was a woman's. She must have been wearing an earring. The other one was obviously a man's, because you can see it was heavily tanned due to continuous exposure to the sun. The rest you know that it was posted yesterday from Belfast. The tell-tale postal mark on the parcel confirms it. The parcel was carefully tied with a sting and knotted. Miss Susan had to cut open it, leaving the knot undisturbed. That gives the only clue now, but I feel it is too early to come to any conclusion."

"I've sent a couple of boys to enquire the medicos," disclosed Lestrade. Homes looked at him and shook his head. "If as you say it was sent by the medicos, they wouldn't have used salt. They would've opted for carbolic or rectified spirit. Besides, see the sprawling handwriting on the address of the parcel. It was written by the one with little education. Not the medicos!" answered Holmes. On hearing Holmes' expertise on chemistry too, Lestrade became dumbfounded!

"There could be more to it. The two could've been murdered before their ears were cut off. Let's wait and see. Meanwhile, preserve the parcel as-is condition. Let me have a word with

Miss Susan," Holmes said and drifted inside followed by Dr Watson as Lestrade took leave and went back to police station. Holmes went past the veranda to the living room, his eyes taking picture of everything in there until he found Miss Susan waiting for them. The duo sat opposite to her as Holmes accosted, "I take it, Miss Susan that you have two sisters, right?" "Yes," she nodded, glancing at the group photo on the mantelpiece. "I am the senior of the three. The other two are Sarah and Mary."

Indicating another photo, Holmes asked, "The photo of your younger sister Mary, taken at Liverpool with this man wearing the Naval uniform of a steward, is he her husband?"

"No, Mr Holmes. It was Fairbairn, a friend of hers. That was taken prior to her marriage with Mr Browner. Incidentally, Browner is also a sailor. He works in the ship called *May Day.*"

"When last did you meet your sisters?" Homes casually plunged in as he got up and began pacing up and down, studying Susan's ears sideways. "Why? yes, we all visit each other. Some time back Sarah went to Mary's house to spend a week with her, but returned after a few days, because there was some misunderstanding between them. It was Browner. A tough guy when he drinks, which is most often." Holmes thanked her and stood up. "I guess a meeting with your other sisters will be useful," he said. Then the two left.

On their way Holmes went to a telegraph office and gave a wire to a young detective friend of his, by name Algar, living at Liverpool, asking him to keep a tab on Mary and Mr Browner there. He gave their complete address also.

Then they took a carriage and went to New Street in Wallington where Sarah lived. But the doctor who answered the door would not let them in. "Miss Sarah is ill. Brain fever! Please come after ten days," so saying he nearly shut the door on their face. By then it was midday. Holmes and Dr Watson went to a restaurant, had their lunch and returned to the hotel room when the clerk at the reception relayed Holmes a telegram.

It was from Lestrade. It said that he (Lestrade) was on to something very hot and urged Holmes and Dr Watson to dash to New Brighton. He added that he had sent a coach for them. Holmes pocketed the telegram, shrugging, "That's it! Detectives have no set timings." Just then a coach pulled up before the hotel. It was from Lestrade.

An hour and a half later the coach reached the spot near a lake at New Brighton. There was a small crowd. Lestrade shook hands with them as he said, "The local police have fished out two bodies. It might interest you." Holmes paused as he quipped, "What do you think I am, a damned undertaker?" On hearing this, Lestrade and Dr Watson burst out laughing.

"What I meant to say was, the two bodies over there," indicating the corpses laid and covered at one corner, Lestrade went on, "It ended up as you have guessed. Each body has a *missing* ear! In other words, these two were murdered before their ears were cut off."

"We expected it, didn't we? It's our hunch. Anyway, we'll know how they had died after seeing the post-mortem report. If they had been murdered before being dumped in the lake, the lake water would not be in their bowl! If it is the other way around, I mean, if they had been forcibly drowned, then this lake water could be lodged in their stomach. Did you enquire the boat club man?"

"Yes. He tells me that these two victims came here three days back that afternoon and hired the boat for a jolly ride, but never returned. They found the boat abandoned. They didn't take it seriously as some people do so to dodge paying extra money for the additional hours of ride."

"Did any one hire the boat after them?" Holmes slipped his catch question.

"Come to think of it, yes Mr Holmes! They tell me that a big man, middle-aged, tall and hefty, with a shaved head, had hired a boat. But unlike these two he returned to the base and went away quickly."

Holmes thought for a while then went to see the bodies. One of the cops there removed the sheet. Bending double, Holmes and Dr Watson studied the corpses. "It seems that these two had succumbed to severe head injuries. Someone should've hit them hard on their head with a strong object. By the way, the body of the woman has the faint resemblance of Miss Susan, hasn't she?" said Holmes as he straightened and moved away. "I've a few hunches, but they require some verification. Well, Mr Lestrade, send me a copy of the post-mortem report. I guess, by that time I'll have it solved," so saying he nodded and headed to the waiting coach, followed by Dr Watson.

The two went to the harbour. There he and Dr Watson spent half an hour and left for the hotel room. The same evening Holmes received a telegram from Algar.

Dear Mr Holmes:

" As directed by you I have gone to the house of Mary, the youngest sister of Miss Susan and found it locked. The neighbours say that Mary had gone out three days ago and did not return since then. Maybe, she was visiting a relative of hers. The house was locked. Her husband Mr James Browner is on duty, now sailing far off. " – Algar.

Holmes was waiting for this telegram only. Upon receipt of it now, he and Dr Watson went out to the telegraph office. There Holmes gave a brief message to Lestrade, telling him that the ship *May Day* would be arriving the next evening and told him to arrest Browner the moment the ship is berthed and take him into custody and that he and Dr Watson would come to the police station to see him.

"Now it is almost solved. We can have a peaceful dinner and sleep," said Holmes. The two took bath and went out for a stroll.

The next evening after receiving a telegram from Lestrade they took a coach and went to the police station. "As informed by you, I went to the harbour and arrested Browner," beamed Lestrade. "I expected stiff resistance from him and was prepared. But surprisingly, he did not even argue. He cooperated very well."

Browner would be any age between 35 and 40. He was tall, hefty with a flat nose as that of a boxer. His head was shaved. He was sitting on a stool at one corner. Holmes and Dr Watson sat before Lestrade. After sipping a hot tea, Holmes asked Lestrade about the cardboard box. At a nod from Lestrade one of the cops who stood guarding Browner, opened the cupboard, took out the parcel and kept it on the table before them.

"Well, it's the knot on the sting that first paved way for the investigation. It's a special knot only sailors can put. Mr Browner is a sailor. So it pointed an accusing finger at him. However, I dug deeply. The more I did, the more it got around Browner. At Susan's house I observed that the cut off female ear in the parcel resembled hers. Hence I wanted to make sure whether her two sisters were alive or dead. Sarah was ill. But my friend at Liverpool told me that Mary who left home about three days before did not return. This endorsed my doubt that she could have been murdered and it was her ear in the parcel.

"Yet, I considered other angles also, because Mary had a friend called Alec Fairbairn at Liverpool with whom she had taken photo before her marriage. He was a steward in the Navy. Thus my suspicion grew on Fairbairn too. But on checking at the office of the ship *May Day,* I came to know Browner's involvement in this case is more. The other day due to technical snag his ship returned to the harbour and he went home ahead of the usual timing. Just then he saw his wife Mary leaving.

"He trailed her and saw her join Fairbairn and together they took a train to New Brighton. It was very snowy there at that time and the visibility was poor. There they hired a boat and went on a jolly ride. Browner, who followed them, also took a boat, intercepted them and hit Fairbairn, first, on the head with the oar. His skull cracked, he died instantly. Browner then did the same for Mary, cut one of their ears and dumped the bodies in the water. Then he sent a parcel of them to Miss Susan's place, obviously to hint them about it all. Why did he commit this double murder is best known to him. Though I have some hunches, let's hear him confess his crime," Holmes said as he finished his tea and kept the empty cup on the table.

Browner quickly swigged the last drop of his tea and spoke up, "It's very interesting to hear Mr Holmes narrate the whole episode as if he had seen it. I admit my crime without any fuss. The trouble started when Sarah had come and stayed with us some time before. I wouldn't approve of her. Most unscrupulous woman I've ever seen. She fell for me. But when I did not reciprocate her lust, she got annoyed and began causing trouble for me. She had put poison in Mary's mind saying that I was no match for her and that Fairbairn was the right man for her."

"Mary started moving closely with Fairbairn. Despite my warning she wouldn't listen. Whenever I set sail, those two met and made merry. As Mr Holmes had said a short while ago, the other day when I went back home ahead of my scheduled arrival, I saw her go out. The rest went on as Mr Holmes concluded. I murdered Fairbairn first. Until then I did not intend to kill Mary. I was ready to condone her. But on seeing her falling on Fairbairn's body and weeping, I couldn't digest. I killed her too. Then cut their ears, shoved the bodies in the water and sent the ears to Miss Susan's place where Sarah was staying at that time. But she had gone back due to sickness. Thus Miss Susan happened to receive it and you all came into the picture."

The post-mortem report also said that the two succumbed to head injuries and only after that their bodies were dumped in the lake.

Sherlock Holmes stood up. And so did the others. Inspector Lestrade thanked Holmes and Dr Watson and added, "Now Mr Holmes, there's another interesting kidnapping case......"

"Which you can handle for time being," completed Homes, smiling as he and Dr Watson came out and walked towards a coffee bar opposite.

The Adventure of The Mazarin Stone

"People say that only changes are constant. But this room and the furniture here remain unchanged right from the day one I stepped in," remarked Dr Watson, his lips twisting down with a smile. He was a good friend and also the trusted lieutenant of master detective, Sherlock Holmes.

"That's because, sir, Mr Holmes is too busy even to throw a second glance and tell me to arrange things," grinned Billy the page boy at the residence of Holmes. Billy was a sincere, hard working and intelligent youth who really cared for his master Holmes. And knowing this, Homes, in turn, had a soft corner for him.

"I guess, I like it that way because my favourite chair is in the usual place," so saying Dr Watson lowered himself in the chair and looked pleased. "Is Mr Holmes resting?" asked he, after a pause.

"Of course, sir. It sounds odd, but you know he has no set timings," replied Billy glancing at the wall clock that showed a little past seven that evening. "During the last two days Mr Holmes had been taking different *avtars*. He didn't have a bite. When Mrs Mason asked him when he would find time for dinner, he said 'Seven thirty the day after.' Thus, he keeps working nonstop. I can see he looks tired and wornout. But he seldom cares about his health. The day before, he roamed under the pretence of a job seeker and yesterday transformed into an old woman," he said indicating the crumpled outfit of an old lady on the sofa.

Dr Watson looked at the outfit and burst out laughing as he suddenly noticed that the only change in the room was some new curtains at every door and window. "Any one coming to see him?" he asked.

"Only a few days back the Prime Minister and the Home Secretary have visited. Then came the Lord Cantlemere......"

"Lord Cantlemere?" Dr Watson's voice shot up unaware. "Jeepers! What on the earth for?"

"Strictly between Mr Holmes, you, I and this big table, it's about the case of the crown diamond."

"Oh, that one hundred thousand pound theft case?"

"That's right, sir. The Prime Minister and the Home Secretary were very nice and kind when they discussed the case with Mr Holmes, but his Lordship looked dogmatic and he doesn't approve the other two dropping the case in the lap of Mr Holmes. However, the other two used their veto and convinced the Lordship. That's it. Since then, Mr Holmes has been busy. And not only that, you'll see one more a*vtars* of Mr Holmes right here." Billy went near the window that overlooked the busy street below and pulled its curtain.

Dr Watson's eyes betrayed his surprise on seeing the life-sized effigy of Sherlock Holmes made to sit in the armchair, with the head tilted down as if he was reading a book. Just then Billy did another amusing thing. He pulled the curtain down and lifted the head of the effigy and set it at another angle as if Holmes had shifted his position. "It's to give an impression to any curious eyes from the road that Mr Holmes is at home while all the time he'll be out chasing a crooked shadow."

"Come to think of it," went on Dr Watson, "It's nothing new to Holmes. Sometime back also we did this trick to pacify the curious eyes of the enemies that Holmes was at home and not pursuing any case."

"People watch from athwart the road, some out of curiosity and some to know his movement. Right now there's one fellow across, gazing nonstop at this window."

Dr Watson went near the window and peered outside. Just then the bedroom door opened and Holmes stepped out. On seeing Dr Watson he made a surprise grunt. Though, as Billy had said, he looked pale and tired, he was active as ever. With the usual springy step he too reached the window, glanced outside and pulled down the curtain as he said, "Okay, Billy, you get off before it's too dark. I'm worried about your safety," then turning to Dr Watson he added, "Just because he's assisting me here, his life too is in peril...."

"Oh God! Who'll want to hurt him and in what way? I've a feeling that you're jumping to conclusion, Holmes," spoke up Dr Watson.

"Not at all. In fact, I'm expecting trouble this evening. It wouldn't surprise me if it turns out to be a murder."

The serious look in Holmes' eyes made Dr Watson to let him have his own way. Meanwhile, Billy took leave. "I guess, we could do well with a pint of alcohol." Minutes later, after the booze, Holmes felt better. "I'm told that you've skipped your meals during the last few days. As a doctor let me tell you, it's not advisable. Mind your health, Holmes."

"These two are my food," Holmes indicated the liquor bottle and his pipe.

"By the way, what about this crown jewel theft case?" asked Dr Watson.

"I was coming to that. Listen, note this name and address of the murderer and pass the buck to Scotland Yard with my love. Name, Count Negretto Sylvius, at # 136, Moorside Gardens, M.W."

After noting down, Dr Watson asked Holmes why could he not arrange for the arrest of this man, Sylvius. "Because, I don't know where they've hidden the diamonds. I mean, the stolen great yellow mazarin stone. There are two men. Another one is called Sam Merton. This morning I wore the disguise of an old woman and fooled him on the streets into guiding me. He carried my sun umbrella and conversed with me in half Italian. I, then, tailed him and saw him go to Straubenzee's work place to buy an air gun, maybe to shoot my dummy made out by our Billy."

At the mention of his name, as if waiting for this moment, Billy came in with a card in his hand and gave it to Holmes. The card carried the name of Sylvius. Holmes passed it to Dr Watson as he said, "That he has called on me shows his steel in character. At the same time, it also endorses that he fears me."

Now the calm situation was gradually turning into seriousness. Sensing the enemy's dragnet closing in on them, Holmes told Dr Watson to take a look outside. Dr Watson did as he was told. "Look, there's a fellow standing and watching the window," he cautioned.

"That must be Sam Merton, an accomplice. The fish now nibbles at the bait. Now, slip out unseen and get the police here. Give the police the letter I gave you. Meanwhile, let me hear what these two have to say."

"Take care of yourself," said Dr Watson as he left the room.

At a nod from Holmes, Billy went out and ushered in Sylvius who was tall, well-built with a springy step of a boxer, wearing neatly pressed dress and neck tie. He should have been a wanderer, for his weather- beaten, sun-tanned complexion denoted it. And as if to cap it all, the long bushy moustache gave him the look of a sheriff of a district.

There was no sign of Sherlock Holmes. Billy indicated a chair to him and went out closing the door after him. Sylvius glanced around and spotted the effigy of Holmes. His eyes suddenly turning hostile, he pulled out the club and was advancing menacingly towards it, thinking that it was Holmes! He went tip-toeing near it from behind, lifted the club and was about to slam a blow on the head when a voice stalled him.

"Hold it, palsy!"

Sylvius spun around on his heels, his eyes taking a swift, sweeping glance around. Then he saw Holmes step out of the bedroom, with a scornful smile. For a brief moment he stood puzzled, then examined the effigy to realize that he was doped.

"I had to make out a dummy one for some customers like you. I've placed an order with a French modeler by name Tavenier. Come to think of it, he's an expert in making wax dolls the way Mr Aw, Straubenzee, the one makes air guns for you," Holmes sounded casual.

For a split second Sylvius was taken aback. But he managed to ask, "What air guns?"

"Take the weight off your feet, will you? Give little rest to your club and the gun. I want to talk to you," Holmes waved him to a chair. "Yeah, that makes two of us. Mr Holmes I want to talk to you, too. Hence I'm here now," spoke up Sylvius.

"Is that right? But, just now an attempt was made by you to break my skull."

"That's because the very sight of you drove me crazy. You and your footloose guys have been sitting on my tail for the past two days now. Yesterday, there was this old sporting man and today, an old woman……"

"With an umbrella which you carried for her," Holmes broke in indicating the sofa on which the umbrella was lying.

"To hell with the umbrella and your disguise! Why this personal attention?"

"Ask yourself, why? My reputation is such that I must know everybody who's anybody. Especially, the outlaws interest me."

"If only I'd known that it were you, you wouldn't be alive now!"

"I could guess that. By the way, I learn that you used to hunt lions in Algeria."

"Does that matter now? I loved fun, thrill, adventure and excitement. It's a sport."

"So, you had a purpose. Similarly, I had one. I want the yellow diamond – I mean the Mazarin stone – you have stolen. Hence, the personal interest towards you. But don't waste time denying it, Sylvius. I know it's with you. And you knew that I know it. So, you called me now just to find out how far I knew about this case! Let me tell you. I know all about it except for one thing: that's where you've hidden it. "

"I wish I knew it, Mr Holmes. Sorry. I don't know what you're talking about."

Holmes regarded him for some time before he went to the table, pulled out the first drawer and took out a small diary like note as he announced, " This note, I would rather put it, is a biography of yours. All your criminal pilgrimages are jotted down here, including your henchmen and other accomplices. To begin with, the fake accident you've created and wiped out one Mrs Harold who was kind enough to remember you in her will, the Blymer Estate, which you've lost in the gamble. Then comes the mysterious death of Ms Minnie Warrender. You were instrumental for her death. Close on the heels of this, you've robbed the Deluxe Express train bound for Riviera dated back Feb. 13, 1892. Thereafter you've forged a cheque and swindled a lot of money on Credit Lyoonnais….."

"Save it, Mr Holmes," addressed Sylvius whose face went pale. "All these are well-cooked stories. But why tell them to me?"

Holmes relit his pipe that had gone dead and continued, "Well, you're a card player, aren't you?"

"What has that one got to do with this?"

"Plenty. What'll you do when the other guy shows up his triumph card?"

"Surrender, of course."

"You learn fast. Do just that. Surrender yourself and let me see what best I can do to save you from going to the gallows. And by doing so, you'll save your friend also."

"Aw, you can't wave a threat that way, Mr Holmes. What's the proof?"

"All that'll be given to the jury. About this crown jewel case also, I've some eye witness account against you two. The two coach men who took you to White Hall and back, and then the commissioner who spotted you loitering near the case, looking suspiciously, as also Ikey Sanders whom you've approached to cut the diamond who got cold feet and refused to budge, but spilled the beans to me. These and many more are there to add to your prolific criminal career. Now, you'll appreciate me, won't you, Sylvius, for having dug up so deep?"

Sylvius face turned ugly and he seemed to be having some trouble in breathing. He appeared like a wolf in a trap. Homes who knew the body language of the one cornered, spoke mildly, "As they say, it's better late than never. Surrender the jewel and save your skin, Sylvius. You know damn well that until I could lay my hands on the diamond, I won't stop at anything. My target is the diamond and not you. Keep it in mind and be reasonable. I won't tell you again."

"I tell you, I don't have that diamond. You're jumping to conclusions. Go ahead and do whatever you want to," Sylvius' voice sounded curt. Shrugging, Holmes pressed the buzzer and when Billy poked his snout in, he told him, "There's a man as amicable as a black mamba standing athwart our house and looking at the window like a star gazer. Chase him in, Billy, will you?"

"Supposing he wouldn't come, sir?" asked Billy.

"He will, if you tell him that his friend Sylvius wants him." Billy nodded and left.

"What are you planning to do with him, Mr Holmes?" enquired Sylvius. "Well," Holmes went on, "Before you came in, I was with my friend Dr Watson. I told him that I'd thrown a bait and that sooner or later I'd catch a shark that really bites. And the shark I'm referring to you is, your friend, Mr Merton."

With an effort Sylvius restrained his patience. Just then the door pushed open and in stormed the hulk of a man. He was tall and hefty with a broken nose that all boxers usually carry and his hands hung loosely as if it would take a swing at any moment that would flatten even an elephant. "Welcome in, Mr

Merton," Holmes accosted mockingly, "I bet it's like waiting at a dentist, standing all day long and watching."

Merton, a bit confused, eyed Holmes and asked Sylvius what it's all about. But Count Sylvius did not speak a word. So, Holmes volunteered, "The game's up, my friend. No more dodging or ducking." But still Merton looked restless. "Speak up," he urged Sylvius, "What's cooking? This fellow sounds funny."

"Of course, I sound funny. It's as they say, pleasure before business. I've narrated all that to your friend. Find out from him. Now let me make it clear for you both. Time is precious to me. I can't afford to waste it with you boys. Let me give you five minutes to discuss and come to a solution. Until then I'll be in my bedroom playing violin. At the end of five minutes I'll come again," so saying he stepped inside his room and closed the door after him. Seconds later, the two heard the violin being played.

"Look pal," Sylvius went on, "Never underestimate Holmes. He knows all about us and our involvement in numerous crimes so far. He's jotted down them in a note book. So, all that he wants from us is the stolen diamond stone. If we give it to him he has agreed to turn his blind eye to us, else he has enough evidence to send us behind the bars for 20 years. He has Ikey Sanders witness too. He now has us over a barrel."

"I don't care a pin. Look, right now he's alone in there. Let me go and finish him."

"Talk sense. He has a gun and he's nobody's fool. It's not that easy."

"Talk in undertone. That fellow must be listening," cautioned Merton. "How can he be with the sound of his violin?" Sylvius answered in a boring voice. "If not him then someone else will. See, there are too many curtains in this room. Somebody must be lurking behind them, can't they?" Merton said as he went to the front window and pushed aside the curtain there when he glanced at Holmes' effigy kept on the chair near the front window. "Wow, this fellow appears to be too dangerous." Sulvius went near it and glanced at the effigy once again.

"That's it. So what shall we do now?" enquired Sylvius. "Keeping the diamond and landing behind the bars is a stupid thing." Merton looked at him sharply. "Do you intend to surrender that stone worth over hundred thousand pound? You're nuts."

As they returned to the hall and were talking they continued to hear the violin being played. Then they heard a sound near the front window. "Who's it?" asked Sylvius.

"Nobody. We just saw. It must've come from the road below."

"Time is running out. I've to think of some alternative," muttered Sylvius as his eyes suddenly narrowed with a thought. "Hey, suppose we strike a deal with Holmes? Let's say that the diamond is with someone else and that it'll take a few days for us to get it. Meanwhile, let's dispatch it through one of our contacts to Amsterdam to cut into four pieces. Our friend Van Seddar can do it. No one knows about him. Somehow we've got to take it to Lime Street and tell him to leave by next boat, however, before Sunday. Let me tell Holmes that the diamond is in Liverpool and thus borrow some time, then give a shake and bolt. How about it?"

"Sounds fine. But where's the stone now?" asked Merton. Sylvius put a hand inside his breast pocket and produced the sparkling diamond. Together they went to the front window where Holmes' effigy was kept and peered at its beauty.

Then it happened!

With the speed and perfection of a striking snake, Holmes leapt up from the chair, grabbed the diamond from them and backed away while his other hand yanked out his gun and pointed it at them. The two were taken by surprise. "Now don't start anything unless you want to stop a bullet. There's a secret passage to this room from my bedroom. I slipped in here, removed the effigy and sat listening to you. The faint sound you both heard didn't come from the road. It's me, shifting my own effigy and sitting down myself. A sort of wait and watch approach. Now it paid dividend. Back up against the wall with your hands up."

The two men remain trapped. However, Merton who couldn't hide his surprise asked Holmes how come he still hear the violin being played. Holmes laughed as he pressed the buzzer, "That's the modern-day gadget. A gramophone!" The next moment the waiting police squad stormed in, frisked them and snatched their guns before they handcuffed Sylvius and Merton and nudged them out. Just then Billy came inside to announce the arrival of Lord Cantlemere. "Send him in,"nodded Holmes.

It was Dr Watson who ushered Lord Cantlemere in. "Most welcome to you honoured, sir." Holmes went up to him, shook hands with him as he touched his coat, "I'm afraid that you'll find it a bit warm inside. May I remove your coat, sir?" he asked courteously. "It's okay, Mr Holmes," smiled the Lord as he lowered himself into the settee. "Hope you've traced the missing diamond?"

"I not only traced it, but also know the one in possession of it right now."

"Do you? If so, what are you hesitating for?" snapped the Lord.

"I await your green signal to arrest the one in possession of it."

"Go ahead. Arrest him," the Lord waved his hand. On

hearing it, Holmes remarked, “In that case, sir, I guess, I've to get a warrant to arrest you.”

For a brief moment the Lord's eyes spat fire as he quipped, “What are you playing at, Holmes? I don't have time for that itsy-bitsy talk.” “You're mistaken, Lord. It's no itsy-bitsy talk. You told me I could arrest the one who is having the stolen diamond, didn't you? Please check your coat pocket!”

Lord Cantlemere put his hand inside his coat pocket and fumbled for some time, then he took it out. The next moment he beamed, his face brightening than the diamond that glistened in his hand and he rose from the seat exclaiming.

Holmes went on to narrate how he had trapped the two and got hold of it. “To make fun of it, I just slipped it in your coat pocket under the pretence of removing it the moment you came in.”

“I appreciate your high sense of humour,” Lord Cantlemere praised him whole heartedly, then he said he wanted to pass the word around among his contacts as how Holmes achieved this impossible.

“It's a pleasure, sir. And it would be a pleasure if you join me for the dinner,” he put in mildly.

Lord Cantlemere expressed his apology and took leave. Just then the smell of frying onions and eggs hit the nostril of Holmes.

“Billy,” called Holmes, “Dr Watson and I are feeling very hungry that we could eat a horse. But that'd be cruel to an animal. So, tell Mrs Hudson that we are ready for dinner.”

The Adventure of The Three Gables

It was a common knowledge among the residents of Baker Street where Holmes lived that at least three to five people visited the master detective with a single purpose: to address their problem to Holmes and seek his help.

But on that breezy, sunny morning Sherlock Holmes and Dr Watson sat talking when a visitor called on Holmes with a different purpose. He was a coloured man, between 25 and 35, solidly built with a flat nose denoting that he had had plenty of punches thrown at him than he delivered. In short, he was as amicable as an ape.

He walked in as dogmatically as if he owned the place and dotted himself before the duo as he accosted, "Who among you is Sherlock Holmes?"

Both the men studied him, then Holmes answered, "If I'm not Holmes, then someone else wearing the outfit of his!" The visitor eyed him for a while like a research scientist studying a new species. "Look Mr Holmes, I didn't come to seek your assistance. I'm here to warn you about one thing: stop poking your snout where it doesn't require. It's just too bad for you. I won't repeat. Understand?"

"Is that all or anything more?"

He went near where Holmes was sitting and extended his clenched fist in front of the nose of Holmes. On seeing it, Dr Watson grabbed the poker and was ready to slam it down on the head of the visitor, for no one had ever behaved with Holmes the way he did. In the past Holmes had encountered many toughies, street fighters, thugs and criminals. He knew he could take two men of his size at a time. So, restraining his patience Holmes smiled mockingly, "Your knuckles didn't turn white. Exert more pressure." "No funny talk, mister. Get it in your thick skull and do what I tell you to."

"I always deal with the one at the top who pulls the sting and not with the puppets like you. Tell me, who do you work for?" "I can't divulge the name. And I know how to soften up trouble makers like you. Yet, I tell you. Lay off Harrow Way. Our friend doesn't want your intervention there. "

Holmes' smile slipped as he said, "You know why I didn't offer you seat? You smell awful. And number two, I know who you are. Your name's Steve Dixie; profession, muscleman; and you were clever enough to remain at large after murdering a young man called Perkins in a brawl outside the Holborn bar. Right?"

Steve reared back and withdrew his hand. His voice suddenly turned acid as he spoke up, "No, sir. It was not me. That fellow was knocked out by someone else."

"You can fool the police, but not me. I know you and your kingpin Barney Stockdale. Now, tell me on whose order are you trying to throw a scare in me ?"

"I apologise, sir. It was Barney who sent me here. I don't know who hired Barney. I just did what Barney told me. That's all!" Holmes studied him. From Steve's body language, especially, his eyes that looked back at Holmes unwinkingly, convinced Holmes Steve was speaking the truth.

"It took sometime for me to dig the fact out of you. Now, get going. The sight of you is sickening." At once Steve bowed and left as if the room was on fire.

Dr Watson dumped the poker and joined Holmes who said, "He's a stooge for Spencer John, the gangster. He is involved in all shady activities. And Barney is the big brain who plans abduction, extortion, beating up people, and Steve is the executioner. Soon after I wound up this Harrow Weald case, I'll turn my attention on to this gang. Now, read this letter," Holmes slipped a paper.

Dear Mr Holmes:

"I'm a familiar stranger to you. It was my late husband, Mr Mortimer Maberley, whom you know as a client of yours. Now I guess. I need your help. It's to do with this house left by my husband. Please make it convenient to meet me anytime tomorrow, will you?

My house, "The Three Gables" is at a stone's throw from Weald Railway Station."

With due regards

Mary Malberley.

After a quick breakfast the duo set off. Of course, the house was close to the station. It was a bit old modelled, stood on the vast expanse of uncared gardens and trees, however, the interior of it was neat and well furnished.

After the formal enquiries, Mrs Maberley, an aged woman with polished manners, spoke of her son, Douglas. On hearing it, Holmes nearly whistled, "Wow, you're undoubtedly a familiar stranger, madam. I knew your son Douglas too. It's ages since we met. How's he now?"

"He's no more," said Mrs Maberley, her voice quivering. Holmes learnt that Douglas had died only recently due to pneumonia. However, the old lady added that prior to his death, he seemed desperate and depressed. When asked if it was a woman or anything, Mrs Malberely showed signs of not willing to go into details about her son's sudden death.

"Tell us, madam, what is bothering you now? We'll do our best."

The lady went on to say that an house agent had called on her the other day and persuaded her to sell this house of hers as it was too big for her and that it was not safe too for her to live in there alone. It made sense. Moreover, as she was looking for a change of scene and wanted to make a tour, she said that she would settle for 500 pounds. The agent instantly agreed to the offer, but added that the buyer wished to purchase the furniture too and told her to name the price for them.

"It puzzled me why did they not try many house nearby which were vacant. And I was reluctant to dispose the furniture. However, I named a price. Again it was agreed to without any bargain.

Yesterday, the agent had visited with the sale deed. Asking for a day's time I consulted my lawyer Mr Sutro. He pointed out that once I signed I wouldn't be able to take anything with me, not even my personal belongings. When I referred this to the agent, he said that a few personal things may be allowed otherwise everything should be left behind or else the deal was off."

Mrs Malberley refused and with that the deal was called off. To Holmes, the deal sounded odd and mysterious. There must be something valuable in this house – valuable to the buyer, of course. Hence, he wanted to buy the house *as-is-where- is* condition like an auction.

Then it happened!

As they were talking, suddenly Holmes motioned them to stay quiet and tip toed to the door, then with one swift moment he pulled the door open and grabbed the arm of a woman lurking behind and shoved her inside the room. She was the servant maid by name Susan. When questioned what she was up to, she said she was just going to ask Mrs Malberley something about lunch. "For that you need not have been lurking for five minutes," snapped Holmes, then turning to Mrs Malberley he concluded, "I take it that you gave the letter addressed to me to Susan to post it. Ask her who she works for?"

"You got it all wrong," Susan denied. When Mrs Malberley pointed who she was talking with the other day over the hedge, she quipped saying that it was no business of hers. Holmes piped in, "You must be passing on the information to someone. Tell me who it is and I'll give you a tenner." Susan glared at them then announced that she was quitting. When she made a move towards the door, Holmes said, "Convey my love to Barney. Tell him his days are counted."

After Susan had gone, they sat talking. Mrs Malberley in reply to a question said that she was living in the same house for two years now. Holmes thought for a while, then stated, "Mind you, there was no offer for two years. Now this agent turned up four days ago and is pressing you hard. Ask yourself why? The previous tenant must've buried a treasure here which they came to know only now. Even then why do they insist on buying the furniture, puzzles me! You never bought any items of value recently, did you?" "No," she said. Holmes then tipped her to ask the lawyer for protection for a few days. "It's just a precaution, that's all."

Holmes got to his feet and took a stroll around the rooms. In one of the rooms he saw a couple of trunks. On being questioned, Mrs Malberley said that they belonged to her son and after his death they were sent to her the previous week. She added that she did not open them yet. Holmes pointed out that one of the trunks must have something important and told her to have them shifted to her bedroom.

When the two walked back to the station, they spotted Steve hanging around. A bewildered expression came on his face at the sight of the two. He gave a wintry smile as he kidded, "Looking for your gun, Mr Holmes?" Holmes replied he was looking for the scent bottle. That hit him where it hurt him. "Look pronto," warned Holmes, "You haven't told me who had sent you. Well, I won't warn you again. I've the dossier called Longdale Pike in which I'd jotted down all about you and your kingpin. All that I've to do is to send them to the cops and that'll doom both of you. Now, mind you, that house, *The Three Gables* is strictly under my care. If anything untoward happened there, I won't spare even your ghost also. Tell that to your filthy-minded boss!"

Despite this warning, a shocking news woke up Holmes the next morning. It said that the house *The Three Gables* was burgled! Holmes and Dr Watson rushed to Harrow Weald. There, in front of the house, a small crowd had gathered and a few cops were moving around briskly. Also present there was Sutro, Mrs Malberley's lawyer. The local inspector sounded that it was an ordinary case of house breaking and that Holmes' expertise seldom required as he knew that it was the handiwork of Barney Stockade and his *aide- de camp* Steve and soon he would nab them.

Meanwhile, Mrs Malberley joined them. She confessed that she did not ask for the lawyer's protection. "It must be Susan, who knew the geography of the house and had tipped the offenders.

Suddenly, someone pressed a hanky on my nose and I became unconscious. On gaining consciousness, I saw a man take out a roll of sheets from my son's trunk. I tried to grab the sheets from him. In the scuffle, I was shoved by another. On hearing the sound my new maid, Mary, rushed up and raised an alarm. Then again I fainted. After coming to surface I found only one crumpled sheet was left by the gang. Rest they've taken with them. I gave it to the inspector."

The inspector grinned as he took out a paper from his pocket and gave it to Holmes, "Not much in there. It's the concluding part of a story by the deceased Douglas." Holmes and Dr Watson glanced at the manuscript. It read:

"......face bled considerably from the cuts and blows, but it was nothing to the bleeding of his heart as he saw that lovely face, for which he had been prepared to sacrifice his very life looking out at his agony and humiliation. She smiled – yes, by heaven! She smiled, like the heartless fiend she was, as he looked up at her. It was at that moment that love died and hate was born. Man must live for something. If it is not for your embrace, my lady, then it shall surely be for your undoing and my complete revenge!"

Holmes indicated the serial no. on this page that showed 245. "What do you make of it, inspector? What happened to the rest of the previous 244 pages? Do you think that the robbers were after this funny novel?" The inspector smiled an all-knowing smile, saying that it seemed queer. Holmes then showed what the inspector had overlooked. "The manuscript that said as a third-person story, suddenly turned into a first-person narration. See, the word *she* became *your* and *he* became *my!* It points to a fact that the writer, Douglas, was addressing his lady love after she had mercilessly dropped him, wasn't he?"

The inspector gaped wordless at Holmes. He cursed himself for overlooking this point. Before he could talk anything further, Holmes left, followed by Dr Watson, assuring that he would call him (inspector) later.

Back on the street Holmes muttered to Watson, "The concluding part of the letter—if my hunch is not wrong—points a suspicious finger at a lady. Now we're going to meet her, a gorgeous woman in the world that any mirror on the wall will underline it. Her name's Isadora Klein. But a most unscrupulous woman in the world! She has a long list of bed partners. After the act, she'll give them brush off. She had married the richest German, a monarch in sugar business. This marriage, after the death of the German, elevated her as one of the richest woman. So her biography goes. Wait and see until you set your eyes on her!"

Minutes later, the coach pulled up before a corner house in the west end at Grosvenor Square.

The bungalow stood majestically amidst well-maintained lawn, tall trees with a fountain in the façade. Briefly, every inch of it boasted her immense wealth and royal taste. There were separate entrances for inmates, visitors and tradesmen. Holmes and Dr Watson were screened at three different locations before a servant who took the card in, returned almost at once saying that Madam was not available. Holmes expected it, took a small paper, scribed, *"Either me or the police. Choose yourself!"* and gave it to the servant. It worked the miracle. Seconds later, the servant ushered them inside the bungalow that looked as if a set was laid for a cinema shooting.

Seated on the settee was Isadora Klein. She looked as elegant as a new fountain pen, with an enviable touch, and stain complexion, buffer-like round face, hazel eyes, straight Grecian nose, celestial lips, square indented chin and long neck that a Miss World would envy. No doubt the very sight of her would make a saint wonder if he had taken any wrong decision in his life. She received Holmes with a broad grin, saying, "I've heard a lot about you Mr Holmes."

Holmes introduced Dr Watson to her. "That makes two of us. I too have heard a *lot* about you, madam," acknowledged Holmes. She nodded, however, her eyes hard as she asked why Holmes had mentioned police in the slip. "That answer to your question lies in your refusing to meet me at first, but budging later on seeing the mention of police, madam! And I'd to drag the police for the obvious reason that your beauty and intellect do not coincide. You've a hired muscleman to throw a scare in me. Listen, I don't get cowed down. Knowingly I took up this risky profession."

"What muscleman? I don't understand what you're saying?" she denied. On hearing it, Holmes got to his feet. "All right, I'll tackle according to my choice."

At once she stood up, forced a smile as she blocked his way. "Sorry, Mr Holmes if I've hurt your sentiments. I admit I've engaged the thugs. I apologise to you. But if you allow me to narrate under what circumstances I had to do that, you'll surely condone me....." Holmes broke in, "Who am I to condone you? I just represent law that will deal with you. At the same time, I want to caution you, madam. Mind you, these thugs have the nasty habits of back-firing the one who engages them!"

"Thanks for the advice, Mr Holmes. But I never involved myself. It's Susan and her husband Barney Stockdale. I've arranged in such a way that these two never knew that I was behind it. They take orders from – well let me tell the truth – from my lawyer. Even then, it's only their words against my lawyer who knows how to wriggle out of it. "

"How about me? How'll your lawyer tackle me if I involve you, Susan and Barney?"

Isadora Klein forced a laugh. "It's time I divulged the whole truth to you. Look Mr Holmes, I may have money, but no security. Men like me for my money and I for company sake. It's just the way I live. Similarly, Douglas was one of them. But he was keen on marrying me! How can I marry a pauper, no matter how handsome he is? Moreover, getting married is not my cup of a tea. So, I got rid off him. But the mad fellow started writing about our close intimacy right from the day one. His idea was to publish a book about our affair. Though he had changed the names, it spoke scornfuliy about my modesty. And from the rest of the details, anyone can easily guess that the woman he had mentioned in his story was me!

"He made out two manuscripts, sent one to me saying that another was for a publisher. I know his publisher. He told me he had not received any mail from Douglas. So, where was it? What'll happen to me if it reached the wrong hand? So, I had to seek outside help to get the second copy. That was the beginning of the sad end of Douglas. After his death, his personal belongings were sent to his mother.

"Hence, in order to get it diplomatically, I came forward to buying her house, including the furniture, knowing that the second copy must be in his trunk. The deal was broke. The old lady, I mean, Douglas' mother, Mrs Malberley, didn't wish to sell her properties. At this juncture, you came into the picture. It was Susan who took the letter addressed to you, read it and tipped to her husband Barney who dared to threaten you through Steve. Finally, having no other choice left, I've arranged to have it robbed. But the fool left the last page there and brought the rest of 244 pages."

"Where are those 244 pages?" Holmes once again interposed.

At once she got up, grabbed the poker and stirred the fire place with a smile, saying that they were reduced to ashes now. "So," she continued, "Tell me Mr Holmes, if you were in my position, what would you've done?"

"If I were you, madam, I wouldn't have started this. Anyway, I have to record my report. And since you're so confident of buying yourself out of trouble, I have nothing to tell you. Those two-Barney and Susan – have to face the heat. Now a personal question: what would it cost to make a global tour?"

Isadora Klein's face lit up as the topic turned away. "Why, around five thousand pounds, Mr Holmes," she replied enthusiastically.

Holmes regarded her for some time then said, "I expect you to give a cheque for that amount to Mrs Malberley. A change of scene would be a solace to her."

"With pleasure," Isadora Klein immediately gave a cheque favouring Douglas' mother.

Holmes and Dr Watson got up. So did she.

"Keep yourself clear of the underworld criminals like Barney. It's said that you can't fool all the people all the time!" so saying Holmes waved a passing coach.

Isadora watched the coach until it turned around the bend. Then she stood thinking, her head bent as if she was realising her sins before she walked in as Holmes' last words kept banging in her ears!

The Adventure of Three Garridebs

Close on the heels of the South African War that called for a cease-fire sometime in June 1902, Dr Watson, who visited Holmes that morning, was told that Sherlock Holmes was sleeping continually for the last two days. Dr Watson knew that it was one of those things as Holmes had no set timings. At times he kept awake for two days and on few occasions like this he slept nonstop for two days.

Sitting in his favourite chair, Dr Watson was glancing at the newspapers when the bedroom door opened and Holmes came out, grinning from ear to ear. After exchanging pleasantries, Holmes gave a rolled up paper to his friend as he said, "If only your name is not Watson and called yourself Garrideb, you'll be in for a great fortune."

"What's in a name?" remarked Dr Watson, smiling. "Plenty," Holmes went on, "I'd rather say it's an odd case. This name Garrideb plays an important role. If you can find a third man with that name, you'll achieve this case. Already, there are two in that name. The one who wrote to engage me is

'Nathan Garrideb, # 136, Little Ryder Street, W.' That's the first Garrideb. The second one is 'John Garrideb, from Moorville, Kansas City, USA,' who is a counsellor at Law, is going to visit us now. If you wait for a little while, you can hear from the client himself...."

Just then the house maid, Mrs Hudson brought in a card. Nodding to her to send the visitor in, Holmes muttered, "Here he comes. Hear what he says!" Holmes said and grinned. Seconds later, a short, well-dressed, powerfully built, middle-aged man, with an air of arrogance, walked in. He seemed restless and so were his eyes, shifting around aimlessly. "Mr Holmes?" he nodded curtly as he sat down and regarded Dr Watson. "Did you get the letter from Mr Nathan Garrideb?"

"Of course, I got it. By the way, you seem to have the British taste written all over you, your dress, coat and shoes," complimented Holmes. "Oh, am I so obvious? Well, it's my business and long stay in England that had a sway in me. Okay, skip how I look and my socks. Now about the letter, what's your next move, Mr Holmes?" enquired John Garrideb, annoyed at Holmes' deep observation.

"Before we discuss the case, I want my trusted friend Dr Watson to be with me. I don't take up any case without his presence. Any objection?" "Suit yourself," shrugged John Garrideb. "Let me brief the whole episode. It all started in Kansas City when Alexander Hamilton Garrideb, a real estate businessman with Midas touch, made millions of US dollars by selling lands and then in wheat business too. And he had invested all that money on lands here, in England. But what was so unique about him was that, he was so fascinated about his name Garrideb that he once approached me to find a man in that name. I pointed out that I was a busy man and refused.

A year later I learned that A.H. Garrideb had died, leaving a fortune to be shared between three Garridebs. Hence, I came into the picture to look for two more Garridebs. But I couldn't find one person of that name. I spread my net and searched in your country. Boy! Am I lucky to find one whose name's Nathan Garrideb? A couple of days back I found his name in the telephone book and called on him. He's the one who strongly recommended your name to me. So I'm here. Please find one more person in that name, Mr Holmes. I'll pay you your fee."

"By the way, since you said you're from Topeka, USA, you might've heard about Dr Lysander Starr, the Mayor there whom I used to correspond with before."

"Sure, Mr Holmes. Though he's no more, his name's still being honoured there."

"Come to think of it, why not advertise in the Agony column in newspapers?" asked Holmes. "Oh, I've done that too. But it bore no fruits," answered John Garrideb in a helpless gesture as he stood up. "Well, Mr Holmes, let both of us keep at it and share our progress. Goodbye."

Holmes watched him go, then turning to Dr Watson said, "Strictly between you and I, Watson I was tempted to take a swing at this fellow, you know? He's full of lies. There was no Mayor I knew of in the name of Sanders. Yet, he said he knew him. And he never gave an ad. in the Agony column in any newspaper, because I keep tabs on that as it is always useful to me. But he said he'd placed an ad. And he is a British though he puts every effort to appear to be an American. Well, I just gave in an impression that he's taken us for a ride. So I didn't cross-examine him.

"Why did he tell lies? What's the motive? There's something serious about it all. Didn't I tell you that it looks odd? I think it's time we turned the heat on. Now let's switch over our investigation from another angle. I want to meet the one who wrote the letter. What's his name? Aw, Nathan Garrideb. Put a call right away, Watson. Tell him that I want to talk to him. "

Moments later, Holmes was talking to him, "Yes, Mr John Garrideb was here. Now I understand the whole set up. Let me do my best. Meanwhile, I wish to meet you and have a word with you. I always make it a point to call on my clients at their residence. It's just the routine stuff. My friend Dr Watson will accompany me. And I wish to meet you alone. So you need not bother to inform Mr John Garrideb, our American Counsellor of Law. Okay? We'll be there tomorrow by 6 p.m. Thank you. Goodbye for now."

Shortly before 6 the next evening, Holmes and Dr Watson entered into the Ryder Street, a small lane that branched off from Edgware road. It was an old modelled Georgian type house, with one window on either side of the entrance. Nathan Garrideb lived in the ground floor, maybe to avoid climbing stairs. The name board denoted that he must have been living in there for quite sometime. A staircase ran up for the first-floor occupants that needed sweeping.

The moment they pressed the calling bell, Nathan Garrideb answered as if waiting for them. He would be any age between 60 and 70, tall, bald, wearing a simple dress. Inside, the house had some odd collections at one throw, very nearly resembling a museum with the dead animals' skull, skeleton, etc. For the next few minutes he went on to explain about his pride possessions. Holmes kept nodding and lifting his eyebrows in wonderment so as not to discourage him.

"You seem to have a varied interest. And that makes two of us. I'm interested in all these. In fact, I starve for time to be with you for a day or two. Anyway, as you're a busy man, I do not want to waste your time. With so much of private commitments you've, I wonder whether you ever go out?" Nathan Garrideb smiled saying that he was too old to wander about and that it interested him to carry out his own experiments. However, he said he occasionally drove to Christie's or Sotheby's as and when he needed some purchase.

When asked about this case, he said, "Mr Holmes, indeed, it thrilled me when the American gentleman approached me and said about finding the third Garrideb and how I'd inherit five million dollars. It was real money I saw only in movie. So, I thought it better to refer it to you rather than going to the police."

"In case you got your share, will you relocate in US?"

"Me? Never. I was born and brought up here. I don't want to relocate. Not at this age. With that kind of money, I intend to expand my research work by hiring some more persons. That's my plan."

"When did this American John Garrideb call on you with the proposal?"

"Tuesday last."

"Did John meet you after his interview with me?" To this question Nathan said that John had met him and briefed about the interview. "John looked a bit annoyed at first, because you said to him that he looked very much like a British than an

American. But before leaving he got over it." When Holmes asked whether John had asked him any money, Nathan said, no. However, when Holmes learned that Nathan had informed John about their visit in spite of telling him not to say, Holmes looked a bit disappointed. By talking to him, Holmes further learned that Nathan Garrideb never had anything valuable among his collection and hence he did not bother about burglary and that he had been living in there for the last five years.

At this juncture, the door swung open and in walked John Garrideb. He looked gay as he waved a paper, "Consider yourself lucky, Mr Nathan Garrideb. Our effort didn't go waste. Here's a guy called Howard Garrideb, the third person with our name. You're a millionaire, now!"

It was an ad. in the paper. And it read:

Howard Garrideb

Manufacturer of Tractors & Farm Equipments, Steam and Hand plows, Drill bits, Reapers, Binders, Harrows, Buckboards and other paraphernalia, as also Estimator of Artesian Wells. Please call Grosvenor Bldg. Aston.

Holmes and Dr Watson glanced at it too, while Nathan Garrideb beamed, praising John. "That paves way for our real wealth," spoke up John, "I've a contact in Birmingham who had sent this ad. cutting to me. In turn, I wrote a letter to this Howard Garrideb that you'll be visiting him tomorrow. It's my suggestion that you go and meet him." But when Nathan Garrideb began saying that such a long journey wouldn't suit to his age and health, John brushed all that aside. "Take me as your inspirer. I've travelled all the way from US just to achieve this goal. So can you. It's hardly 100 miles. Leave home around 2 p.m. You can come back before midnight," he told him, then giving a curt nod to Holmes and Dr Watson, he left.

Holmes gave Nathan Garrideb some time before he expressed his wish of seeing some of the odd collections there. "Sure, Mr Holmes, I know that you're versatile. I'll explain myself," volunteered Nathan. But Holmes told him that he need not bother about it as every item had been neatly showcased and tagged that he would come the next day and look for himself. "If so, Mr Holmes, please collect the key from Mrs Sanders at the basement before 4 p.m. as you know I'll be away tomorrow. I'll put a word to Mrs Sanders."

"I like the place here, calm and peaceful. Your house agent, indeed, has a good taste. By the way, who's your house agent?" Holmes made it so casual. Yet, it took Nathan Garrideb by surprise. He said, "It's Holloway and Steel at Edgware Road. Why, does it really interest you?"

"We seem to have a common taste. My profession requires to broaden my knowledge about archaeology too. I presume that this house is Georgian type."

"That's right," Nathan nodded. Holmes and Dr Watson stood up, spoke briefly then took leave. On their way back, the two went through Edgware Road, but the agent's office was closed. So they returned home.

Back home, Holmes lit his pipe and began pacing up and down as Dr Watson kept the conversation going, "One thing,

Holmes in the newspaper ad. I noticed the word *Plough* had a different spelling. It was *Plows*."

Holmes paused pacing as he smiled. "Not only that. The word Buckboard also. It has American touch all right. But why? It must have been placed by John Garrideb intentionally with the American spelling to fool all of us as if it was placed by an American called Howard Garrideb. But why he insisted that Nathan to visit Birmingham tomorrow? Instead, he could've arranged a meeting here. Again the obvious move, as I guess, is to shift Nathan for a few hours from his residence. I've some hunches. If what I think is true, then we'll see a twist in the whole episode tomorrow."

The next morning Holmes left home a bit early. And he returned only in the afternoon. It was while eating his lunch with Dr Watson, he said, "I'm on to something hot. This morning I went to Scotland Yard and our friend Inspector Lestrade rendered his best cooperation. I dug for the details in the Crime Record Bureau. There it was—the photo of John Garrideb, an ex-criminal. His photo and finger print were there. His original name's Evans, better known in the underworld as Killer Evans." Taking a small paper from his breast pocket, Holmes read it, "Like Hindu Gods with many nomenclatures, our American lawyer has many names: More Croft alias James Winter alias Killer Evans, 44 years, origin Chicago, arrested for having gunned down three men in USA, and it was while serving sentence escaped! Rumour has is that he had some political backing. Emigrated to London in 1893. Two years later, again while playing cards in a club at Waterloo Road, he'd shot another by name Rodger Prescott, a white-collared criminal."

Holmes paused to relight his pipe that had gone dead and continued, "This landed the trigger-happy killer Evans in jail. Eight years later, in 1901 he came out and was under spot light by the police, so kept himself out of trouble. That's Evans criminal pilgrimage. According to the police, he's most notorious, always tucked a gun in his hip and never hesitated to shoot! Thereafter, I called on the house agent of Nathan Garrideb. Remember, Nathan had told us that he has been living in there for five years now? Here's a link to another criminal conspiracy. The house agent told me that prior to Nathan moving in there about five years ago, it had been occupied by a man called Waldron. His description matches with that of the slain Prescott. Now what do you make of it?"

"Isn't it a bit confusing, Holmes?" Dr Watson batted his eyelids. "Not at all, Watson. See, Waldron and Prescott are one. His actual name's Prescott. To the house agent, he had lied that his name was Waldron. Mind you, five years before he was occupying the house in which Nathan lives in."

"So what? Does it matter where Prescott lived prior to his death?"

"I guess so, Watson. And there's some mystery there in the house. Hence, John Garrideb, looking for an excuse, sent Nathan away under the pretence of dispatching him to Birmingham. I smell a rat. And it's worth investigating. This afternoon let's go to Nathan's house, collect the key from the lady Mrs Sanders and spend some time in there. We may be lucky to stumble on to the fact."

Shortly before 4 p.m. Holmes and Dr Watson reached Nathan's house, collected the key from the lady and went inside. Minutes later, Holmes saw her car had roll out. Then working quickly he went on examining the room and the fossils on display and found nothing suspicious. Just then they heard the approaching footsteps. At once they moved to the corner and hid themselves behind the giant cupboard there.

John Garrideb alias killer Evans stormed in by using a master key, and stood looking around for sometime before he went to the table at the centre of the room, and shifted it aside. Taking out a knife he cut the carpet and rolled them aside, then dusting, he pocketed the knife and took from the coat pocket a small crowbar with which he heaved a portion of the wooden plank up. Alas! The next moment there was a dark, gaping hole like a cave, wide enough for two men to sneak in simultaneously. Evans seemed to have brought with him all the tools. This time he produced a candle and match, lit the former and holding it across the chest, he slowly descended the dark steps.

From behind the cupboard both men saw what John was up to. Nodding to Dr Watson to follow him, Holmes got up and gingerly approached the cave-like opening. But the age-old wooden floor creaked under their weight! The next moment Evans' head bobbed up above the opening. Meanwhile, Holmes and Dr Watson, knowing his reputation, pointed out the guns at him. For a split second Evans' eyes betrayed his surprise, however, his built-in instinct to anticipate the unexpected took over and he instantly forced a smile.

"That's the speciality of sleuth Sherlock Holmes." With the fixed grin still on, he scrambled out and dusted himself, aware that two guns were pointed at him. "Well, Mr Holmes, you win. Here, take the candle," he spoke up and his movements were casual as he stretched the candle while suddenly his right hand yanked out his gun and fired two shots. One went scraping Dr, Watson's thigh and he screamed. Holmes reaction was instantaneous. Like a lightning he clouted the butt of the gun on Evans' head. His eyes rolling back, Evans collapsed on the floor.

Holmes grabbed his gun, whirled around, got to his feet and scooped up Dr Watson and carried him to the bed and laid him on it. "Watson," his voice quivered, obviously worried, "Are you hurt? Won't you tell me you're fine?" he said as he rolled up the pant of Dr Watson who, in that brief moment, realised how much Holmes cared for him. So, he said, "Nothing, Holmes. I'm all right. It's the bullet that gouged a portion of the flesh in my thigh." Holmes quickly grabbed a piece of cloth and tied it over the wound to stop the bleeding.

Evans stirred and opened his eyes. Clutching his head, he propped himself against the table. Holmes was burning with rage as he said morosely, "It's your good luck that my friend was not seriously wounded, or otherwise I would've butchered you. Speak up man. What have you got to say now?"

"Sorry, doc. I didn't mean to kill, but to stun you both and flee." Evans cut a sorry figure. "But this Alladin's cave, what were you exploring in it?" asked Holmes. Evans breathed heavily before he muttered, "Well , since you've all the aces up your sleeve, you'd better look for yourself." Holmes glanced inside the opening. He saw parts of dismantled machines, rolled out special papers that were a bit soiled now and then neatly stacked bundles of currencies, etc.

"Well, you were the one denting the country's economy by running this fake currency racket, weren't you?" "Not me, Mr Holmes. It was Prescott, the big brain behind it," confessed Evans.

"Yeah, and you were part of it. You knew what he was up to. So, after killing him you desperately wanted to lay your hands on this, but didn't get a chance as Nathan the occupier of this premises seldom went out. Hence you dreamed up this 'Three Garrideb' story and shifted him momentarily to Birmingham to take possession of these. But we've spoilt your chances of becoming a millionaire. That's it, isn't it?"

"Look Mr Holmes, after coming out of jail, I never harmed anyone. There are two thousand pounds in those two bundles. You both help yourselves and allow me to beat it. It's a deal."

"You're good at bargaining. Even when breathing your last, you'll strike a deal with the God of death, won't you? Lay off this fake currency. The cops know what to do. Now, to settle the score with you for having dared to injure my friend, I'll charge you on attempt to murder. You can convince the judge and speak your way out," Holmes quipped, then turning to Dr Watson he told him to call the Scotland Yard boys. Minutes later, the Scotland Yard police barged in and crowded Evans. Evans looked at Holmes and said with a tinge of hurt, "Only recently I returned from jail. Now you're sending me back again."

"Wish you many more returns of the day," Holmes said and they all laughed at it. One week later, Dr Watson recovered from the bullet injury. But it was the poor, aged Nathan Garrideb whose reverie broke down, and unable to bear the disappointment, fell sick and was admitted in a nursing home.

Retold By – M K Parthasarathy